EVERY LOVE STORY HAS TWO SIDES...

BETSEY'S STORY

The most incredible thing of my life happened to me the first week of school this year...

Betsey's just been named the first girl sports editor of the *Gaz*, her school newspaper. And she's determined to show everyone she's the *best* editor ever! But things start going wrong right away. She's working so hard that she isn't having any fun. And a boy named Eric isn't making her life any easier.

Eric's the new sports photographer—who doesn't know and doesn't care about sports! And he keeps giving Betsey a hard time.

So why can't she get him out of her mind?

TWO BY TWO ROMANCES™ are designed to show you both sides of each special love story in this series. You get two complete books in one. Read what it's like for a girl to fall in love. Then turn the book over and find out what love means to the boy.

Betsey's story begins on page one of this half of *Change Of Heart*. Does Eric feel the same way? Flip the book over and read his story to find out.

3

TWO BY TWO
ROMANCE™

Change of Heart

Patricia Aks

WARNER BOOKS

A Warner Communications Company

Two By Two Romance™
is a trademark of Riverview Books, Inc.

WARNER BOOKS EDITION

Warner Books, Inc.,
666 Fifth Avenue,
New York, N.Y. 10103

 A Warner Communications Company

Printed in the United States of America

First Warner Books Printing: November, 1983

10 9 8 7 6 5 4 3 2 1

Change of Heart

BETSEY'S STORY

Chapter One

The most incredible thing of my life happened to me the first week of school this year. I, Betsey Noble, a junior at Southfield High, was officially elected sports editor of the *Gaz*, our high school newspaper. I can't stand people who are conceited, but I have to tell you, I made history—in two ways. First, the job has never gone to a junior—usually, only seniors are considered worthy—and second, it's absolutely *unheard of* for a girl to be sports editor. Copy chief, book editor, managing editor, even editor-in-chief, but *never* sports editor. The whole thing was a fluke, but my father insists I was born for the job. I have to agree.

For starters, I was raised in a family of jocks. My father went through college on a basketball scholarship. Before he graduated, he was approached by scouts for the Detroit Pistons to join their professional team, but he decided he'd rather be a salesman and not have to worry about torn ligaments and broken fingers all his life. Now he's chief manager of an auto parts store, but he's still crazy about sports. He's given up team games, but he's a terrific Saturday afternoon golfer.

My mother, who looks like a dancer, was actually a championship figure skater. She was considered Olympic material at one time, but says she had no regrets about giving all that up to be a full-time mother. As she puts it, "Training for the Olympics is so demanding that I decided if I had to get up at six in the morning, I'd rather be taking care of a baby than spending hours perfecting a difficult spiral turn." Sometimes I think she must still wonder if she could have made it to the Olympics, though.

My brothers are sports freaks, too. John, who is now a freshman at the University of Michigan, was star quarterback at Southfield High for three years. He's already in training for the junior varsity at Michigan, where he's taking pre-law courses. His dream is to be a lawyer for athletes, and he says he's studying the field "from the ground up."

My kid brother, Rick, is a nonstop mover

and talker. The only time he shuts up is when he's in the water, which is where he spends most of his waking hours. The swimming coach says he's the Mark Spitz of the thirteen-year-olds, and if he stays with it, he should swim off with some medals of his own.

Because of my parents' and brothers' dedication to athletics, it never occurred to me that sports wasn't an important part of everyone's life. I've been dragged to events from the time I could walk. Besides basketball, I've seen a zillion baseball, football, soccer and hockey games, tennis matches, swimming meets, and even auto races. By the time I was ten, I knew the differences in the layup, the hook, the jump shot, or the overhead in basketball. And when someone mentioned stick-handling the puck at the sideboards, I knew they were talking about hockey. While most kids were reading the funnies, I was always more interested in the sports page. So without even trying, I've learned a lot of details that would qualify me for the job of sports editor.

The other requirement, of course, was being able to write. To be perfectly honest, I'd rather do creative writing, especially poetry, than straight reporting, but I love working on the *Gaz*. Last year I was a cub reporter and covered mostly sports events. Mr. Loomis, our faculty adviser, and Scott Palmer—the then sports editor—were impressed with how much I knew about sports. Scott, who was

3

cute, but not exactly dedicated to his job, made me his unofficial assistant and dumped a lot of stories on me. Actually, I didn't mind because I got a by-line with each story, and I loved seeing my name in print. I also got a lot of experience, which didn't hurt when I was being considered for the editorial job this year.

Everything worked in my favor, including fate. Jeff Stone, a good writer and a sports nut, had been elected by the staff. The editorial lineup was announced in the issue just before summer vacation, and my name was to be listed on the masthead as one of thirty reporters. I was glad to find out that I would be assigned more feature stories in the coming year.

Then, in August, Jeff learned that his father was being transferred by his company, and the whole family was moving to Hong Kong for a year. That meant that someone had to fill the vacancy he was leaving on the paper. So as soon as school began, Mr. Loomis called for an emergency meeting of the staff in the *Gaz* office to choose a new sports editor.

I've always been a little intimidated by Mr. Loomis, who is a legend in our school. In addition to being adviser for the *Gaz*, he teaches senior English and has a reputation for being Southfield's toughest but most inspiring teacher. I think he got his idea of how to run a paper from some old movies and thinks of himself as a crusty curmudgeon who should be wearing a green eyeshade and suspenders. He does take enormous pride in the *Gaz*. and his standards are not easy to meet. So when he approves a story I've written by simply saying, "Not bad," I feel as though I've been nominated for the Pulitzer Prize. On the other hand, if he looks at me sideways over his horn-rimmed glasses and mumbles, "Needs work," I really feel like I've let him down. I soon learned that I'm not the only one who feels that way. Although Mr. Loomis insists that the *Gaz* is a student-run paper, he has more influence than anyone else, of course.

Mr. Loomis does not show favoritism, though, and I considered myself lucky that my stories were blessed with more "not bads" than "needs works." On the other hand, he never singled me out for any special praise, either. That's why I was surprised when it came time for the staff to elect someone to replace Jeff, and he gave me the shortest but probably the strongest campaign speech on record.

Adam Winslow, the brainy, no-nonsense editor-in-chief, conducted the meeting the second day of school and asked for some nominations. Several names—all boys'—were mentioned and greeted with mild enthusiasm. Jeff was such a natural for the position that he was a tough act to follow, and no one seemed to measure up. Finally, Adam turned to Mr. Loomis and asked him to make a suggestion.

"You couldn't go wrong with Betsey Noble," he said without hesitation.

I hadn't been too interested in what was going on, so hearing my name really jolted me. It seemed to shock everyone else too, and there was an outburst of comments—not all exactly flattering. "A girl!" someone shouted, with undisguised chauvinism. "Why not?" someone else—a girl—replied. "That's breaking tradition." "It's about time!" "A female sports editor? No way!" "It's time we came out of the Dark Ages." "It's okay for a British prime minister." "That's different." "Why?" "Because." "She's only a junior." "Who? The prime minister?" "No, dummy."

The noise level of the voices was rising as the intelligence level of the conversation was sinking. Adam pounded his fist on the desk and asked for quiet. "Enough!" he shouted. "Let's get the voting going. One at a time, come up to my desk and write in your choice of those who have been nominated." He waved a plain white memo pad in the air. "Fold it once, drop it in this basket beside the desk, and return to your seats. We'll tally the results immediately."

As soon as he finished, everyone started talking at once, and again Adam asked us to knock it off. "No more electioneering, only one vote per person, and may the best man—oops—or woman win."

There was a flurry of applause, but then

everyone settled down, and the voting went on pretty quietly.

Until that moment, it had never occurred to me that I would be a candidate. I was flattered that Mr. Loomis had tossed my hat in the ring, but I thought that would be the end of it. Just being mentioned was a major breakthrough, and I thought how amazed my brothers would be. As I stood in line waiting to vote, I thought of how I'd tell the story when I wrote to John. I had already composed my first sentence: *You'll never believe it, but yours truly was nominated for . . .*

"Next," Adam said, shoving the pad in front of me.

I filled in my name, thinking that I was at least guaranteeing myself one vote, and went back to my seat. Sara, a beautiful blond senior who had been elected managing editor—and who had never spoken one word to me—brushed by my chair and whispered, "I voted for you."

"You what?" I asked idiotically.

"It's about time we broke down the barriers. Besides, you're a good writer."

I was amazed, and before I could find my voice she had walked off. That's two votes, I thought, and continued imagining my letter to John.

Adam had assigned two kids to sort out the votes, and I was still figuring out my letter when he again demanded our attention. There were four piles of paper on his desk, one thicker than the others. I expected the winner to be Steve Weiss, a fair writer, but a good all-around athlete, and very well liked. If I hadn't been running, I would have voted for him myself.

"The winner of this election, by a landslide," Adam said, as though he were announcing the results of a presidential election, "is . . . Betsey Noble."

I was so stunned that I'm not quite sure what happened next. I vaguely remember a loud roar and a bunch of kids milling around, offering me their congratulations. I floated home in a zombielike state, revising in my mind my letter to John. *You'll never believe it, but yours truly was elected . . .*

When I got home, my mother was trimming the privet bush that lines the walk to our old Victorian house on Mulberry Street.

"You look like you've got good news," my mother greeted me as I ran up the walk and kissed her on the cheek. I'm never good at hiding my feelings no matter how hard I try, and I couldn't stop smiling.

"I'm the new sports editor for the *Gaz*," I blurted out.

"You're *what*?" My mother dropped the pruning shears.

"Sports editor," I repeated. Then it all came out in a rush. "You see, Jeff Stone had to go to Hong Kong, and someone had to fill his place, and even though I thought Steve Weiss would be elected, Mr. Loomis suggested me, which is why—''

"Betsey," my mother interrupted, "that's fabulous! I can't wait to tell Daddy." She hugged me, and I knew she felt just as good as I did about the news. I broke away to call my friend Robin.

I went into the house and dumped my things in my bedroom. Practically every square inch of the walls is covered with posters of sports events. From the look of my room, no one would ever guess that my secret passion is writing poetry.

In a small gable between my bedroom and John's is a telephone. And now that John's off to college, it's practically my very own private line. Robin and I have to talk on the phone at least once a day, even if we've seen each other in school.

Robin Bennett is my best friend, and has been since *before* we were born. We're convinced of that, because our mothers became friends at a natural childbirth class, had the same midwife, and even shared the same hospital room when we were born—four hours apart. We both weighed in at a little over seven pounds, and our weight has been almost identical ever since, although at 5'5'', I'm an inch taller. That's why, at 112, Robin is always trying to lose two pounds, even though her figure is perfect. She has short, curly black hair, a turned-up nose, a big smile, and hazel eyes. I have wavy light brown hair, green eyes, and an ordinary nose.

Robin is very musical. She sings, plays the guitar, and couldn't care less about sports. And she admits that she goes to the Southfield football games strictly for social reasons. I, on the other hand, can hardly carry a tune, was a complete failure at learning the guitar chords that Robin patiently tried to show me, and take for granted that I'm a natural athlete.

Sometimes I think the reason we're so close is that we're never competing in the same field. When the choral conductor, Mr. Blade, picked Robin to sing a solo at the spring concert last year, I was just as excited as she was. That's why I knew she'd be equally excited for me when I told her about the *Gaz* job.

Sneakers, our dog who thinks he's a person, settled himself next to me on the windowseat while I dialed Robin's number. She doesn't have her own phone, but since half the calls in her house are for her, no one else in her family answers the phone. So before she finished saying hello, I told her about my triumph.

"Congratulations!" she screamed. "You're *perfect* for the job!"

"Thanks," I said, doubly happy now because she was so happy for me.

"You must be thrilled. You've made history, you know, What a responsibility!"

Responsibility. That word gave me butter-flies. I hadn't yet faced the kind of nitty-gritty work my new job would involve.

"Hey, Betsey, you still there?" I'd been silent for so long that Robin wondered what had happened to me.

"I'm here," I said, "but you just reminded me of something."

"What?" Robin sounded confused.

"To tell the truth," I confided, "I'm a little scared."

"Why should you be? You won the election fair and square, and Mr. Loomis campaigned for you."

"I know, but now I've got to live up to what everyone expects of me."

"Don't worry. You're a terrific writer, and you know more about sports than my kid brother."

"Who knows almost as much as *my* kid brother."

"Who knows almost as much as my *father*."

"Who know almost as much as *my* father."

"Who knows almost—"

By then we were both laughing so hard that we had to stop. "Later," Robin sputtered, and hung up. I was still laughing when I returned to my room, Sneakers nudging me along. But now the reality of what I had to do hung over me like a black cloud. The only way I could make it go away would be to show that I was not only a *good* editor, but the *best* sports editor the *Gaz* ever had.

Chapter Two

The next couple of days were a shakedown period for the new *Gaz* staff. I knew how things worked from last year, but back then all I had had to do was get my own story in on time. Now I had to assign stories, make sure everyone met their deadlines, edit and proofread their material, choose pictures, and write captions and headlines. If there were mistakes, I'd have to answer for them. If I failed, I honestly thought I'd be setting women's liberation back for years. I could easily work myself into a panic just thinking about it, a feeling I'd never had before in my whole life.

Schoolwork has never thrown me. I'm certainly not a brain, but I've always gotten good grades, especially in English, my best subject. I've always been able to keep up with my homework, so I don't usually panic before an exam. My friend Mary thinks studying every day is a waste of time, so she pulls an all-nighter whenever we have an exam and manages to do pretty well. Of course, she's wiped out for the next couple of days, and I've tried to convince her there's an easier way. She argues that she can only operate well under pressure. When I discovered that the first issue of the *Gaz* had to be ready in three weeks, I envied her.

I decided I couldn't let on about how insecure I felt, so I decided to try to act tough, even though it wasn't really my style. I figured I had to assert myself and take a hard stand on every issue, so that people would take me seriously. I started putting my plan into action at our very first meeting.

We were gathered around one end of a conference table, deciding which stories to include in the first issue. There was no question that the year's first football game would have priority. There would be an interview with Chip Hopkins, the star quarterback and all-American heartthrob, plus a rundown on the cheerleaders and an article on the volleyball team.

"Let's get a cartoon in there someplace," Adam suggested.

"Good idea," Danny said, grinning. "I

happen to have a whole notebook full you can choose from." Danny is a really funny guy who looks normal but draws outrageous cartoons.

"Do you have anything on football, volleyball, or cheerleading that could tie in with our stories?" Sara asked.

"Some of each," Danny replied. "And I can always draw to order."

"Terrific," Adam approved. "Agreed, Betsey?"

Probably because they hadn't asked my opinion sooner, I said no. Even though I'd always loved Danny's work, I didn't want to give in. "I think we'll need every inch of space for the football story," I said.

"Is that because you're writing it?" Danny smiled at me, but I knew he was serious.

"No," I defended myself, "it's because I think the story is more important than a cartoon."

"But endless columns of type can turn the reader off," Adam said. "We don't want to bore our readers, Betsey."

"My story won't be boring," I asserted.

"Didn't mean that," Adam explained. "It's just that a page is more appealing if it offers more than straight type. A cartoon would be the perfect solution."

"Especially one of Danny's," Sara added.

"Are you suggesting Danny's cartoons are more important than my article?" Why was I overreacting?

"Not at all," Sara said. "There should be room for both, that's all."

"Well, you wanted to know my opinion, and I gave it to you," I said, "I thought as sports editor, I could decide and that would be that."

"You don't understand," Sara pointed out. "Everyone's ideas are welcome, Adam is editor-in-chief, so he makes the final decision. For really major things, we turn to Mr. Loomis. Whether we include a cartoon or not is not major, so it's up to Adam."

"If it's up to Adam, then I don't see why you bothered asking me." I knew I was sounding like a two-year-old, but I couldn't seem to back down from the stupid position I'd taken.

I saw Adam and Sara exchange a raised-eyebrow look, which made me feel like a total nerd. There wasn't much more I could say. I'd taken a stand, and I had to stick with it. Sara then started asking Adam about what kind of typeface he thought would be good for the front-page headlines, a discussion which definitely excluded me. I wasn't sure whether I should feel insulted or relieved, but I took the opportunity to return to my desk at the far end of the room.

As I started to walk away, Danny spoke up. "If it were up to me, I'd do a huge cartoon of a female sports editor—a pretty girl made out of words with a typewriter for a heart."

"That would really grab the reader," I

growled, and quickly turned away before he could get in the last word.

I sat down at my desk and concentrated on the questions I thought Chip should be asked for the interview that was scheduled to take place in the *Gaz* office the next day after school. Adam had advised me earlier to let one of the staff reporters handle the interview.

"You can work up a lot of the questions, but it's not necessary for you to do the actual interview. You ought to give Lizzy a crack at it. She told me that was the one assignment she would die for."

Lizzy was a frizzy-haired tenth-grade cub reporter who was still pretty inexperienced. The thought of having Chip all to herself for an hour, even just for business, was probably the most exciting thing in her life. I didn't want to take away her big moment, so I had told Adam I'd think about it. But now I decided I didn't want anyone telling me what to do. I decided then and there that I would do the interview myself. I did feel a little guilty about disappointing Lizzy, but I could live with that more easily than with thinking I'd let myself be pushed around.

I had all my questions ready for Chip when he appeared in the office the next day. He was in his football uniform and looked like a combination of Superman and an athlete in a Wheaties ad. I could see why girls flipped for him, even though he really wasn't my type. In my book, there's such a thing as being too rugged. But every female eye followed him as he stopped at Adam's desk, chatted with him briefly, and then came over to where I was working. He moved some papers away from the corner of my desk and settled his hulk on the edge. "I'm Chip Hopkins," he began, "as if you didn't know."

"And I'm Betsey Noble."

"I've heard about you, Betsey. You're a first for me—first female sports editor I ever had to cope with."

"Forget about that and let's get started." I pulled a portable tape recorder out of my bottom drawer and flipped the *on* switch.

"Hard to forget you're a girl," he remarked, "but we do have to get started. I promised Coach I'd be on the field for practice in a half hour."

"That's not nearly long enough. I have at least an hour's worth of questions." I had trouble not sounding annoyed.

"Betsey, this is only the beginning," he said with a wink. "You can come with me to practice, you can talk to me afterwards, you can even let me take you out for a Coke sometime."

"Okay," I said. I didn't like his attitude, but at least we'd have enough time for a good interview.

"But if you don't mind me saying so, this is the worst possible place for an interview. It's too noisy. Even my deep voice won't record properly with all this competition. Why don't we split this scene and head for the field?''

Without waiting for my answer, he slipped off my desk and waited for me to stand up.

I knew his idea made sense, so I dumped the tape recorder, a pad and some pencils in my canvas book bag and led the way to the door. I stopped at Adam's desk and explained to him that it was too noisy to have a decent interview in the office.

''I see you're not letting Lizzy in on this,'' Adam said.

''Not this time,'' I said, feeling another pang of guilt.

''It's up to you,'' Adam remarked. His voice was neutral but I could tell he didn't approve.

''One problem though, Adam. We should have some pictures. Can Greg come out later and take some shots?'' Greg was the roving photographer for the paper, and I assumed he would be available.

''Greg doesn't have time to cover sports. He's too busy with every other section of the paper, so Mr. Loomis is going to send out word that we're looking for a sports photographer.''

''You mean there'll be one person just to shoot sports? That's terrific.''

''I thought we were in a hurry,'' Chip called to me from the door.

"I've got some good news. We're going to get a photographer just for me," I said happily.

"Glad you approve of something," Adam mumbled, as he pushed his chair back from his desk, stood up, and turned away.

"Come on," Chip urged. "At the rate we're going, I'll miss practice altogether."

"O.K., O.K.," I said.

It was easy to pretend I hadn't heard Adam's remark, but there was no way to avoid Lizzy's stare. She was standing right next to the door— had she purposely planted herself there?—and shot me a look of hurt and hate that shook me up. She'd never understand that my reason for doing the interview myself was my fear of giving up any power and that I wasn't the least bit interested in Chip. But dwelling on Lizzy's problem was a waste of time. The important thing was to get a good interview.

On our way to the field, I took the tape recorder out of my bag and started asking Chip questions. I got the standard ones out of the way first: "When did you first play football?" "Do you plan to go out for the team at college?" "Is it true you've already been scouted by some universities?"

Then, without being aware of it, I guess I started using a lot of technical sports language.

"When you have an option play, how do you decide whether to pass or run or keep the ball to yourself?" Chip looked amazed that I knew enough to ask that question, but he recovered quickly and seemed really excited as he answered.

"Instinct. Depends how the play develops, but I have to make the decision in seconds."

"You're famous for the tackle slant. Can you explain why?"

"It's a matter of split-second timing. I practiced whirling at the snap and jamming the ball into the running back's belly until I got it perfect."

"Last year at the final game on third and long, weren't you taking a chance on an interception when you threw into a crowd of defensive players?"

"Sure, but it was worth the risk. We went on from there to make the deciding touchdown."

We had reached the bleachers, but before we could sit down or I could ask any more questions, Coach saw us and yelled at Chip to take some laps around the field.

"We just got started," I groaned. "I have a zillion more questions."

"No problem, Betsey. I'll give you all the answers you want. If you hang around, we can pick up on it after practice. You're into my favorite subject you know, *me*. And you know a lot for a girl."

"Sorry, Chip, I can't hang around here waiting for you. I've got work to do back at the *Gaz*.

"If you say so," he said in disbelief. "But you'll be the first girl who ever resisted me."

I couldn't afford to say what I was thinking, that I wasn't doing this interview to give him an ego trip. I did admire his athletic ability, but I could have lived without his attitude. I probably was the only girl at Southfield High who didn't think of him as a romantic possibility. On the other hand, I didn't want to make him mad at me and blow the interview, so I kept my mouth shut.

When I got back to the office, I went directly to my desk and typed up what I'd taped. I'd done only a couple of paragraphs when Patsy, a peppy ninth-grader who hung around the *Gaz* as a glorified gofer—her main job was to sharpen pencils and run errands— bounced over to me and started asking questions.

"What's he really like?" she began.

"I don't have time now," I answered. I really did want to get everything down right away so I'd have time to sort it out before our next interview.

"But is he nice?" she asked.

"He's O.K." I had to rewind the tape, because Patsy had been talking and I couldn't listen to two things at once.

"Does he have a girlfriend?" she continued.

"*I don't know*, Patsy," I snapped. "I didn't get around to asking him, the interview isn't finished yet, and if you keep quizzing me it never will be."

"I just wanted to find out what you thought

21

of Chip so I could tell my friends," she explained, pouting.

"If you leave me alone now, I promise you'll be one of the first to see the final column. And you can tell your friends they can read all about him in the first issue."

"Oh, forget it," she muttered and backed off, while I went back to my typing.

When I finished typing up all the material I'd taped, I worked on getting it in order and on tightening up the sentences. It was almost five when I took a breather and noticed that everyone was getting ready to leave.

There was a lot of kidding around, mostly about how it was probably easier to get out a daily city newspaper than it was to publish the *Gaz* once a month

"My uncle's a reporter for *The Detroit News*," Adam told everyone, "and he says the only way to keep your sanity is to think of the whole thing as a joke."

"At least he's getting paid for it," someone remarked.

"Yeah, it's not a bad way to make a living," said another.

"Especially if you have a screw loose somewhere."

Then they all started laughing, but personally I didn't find the situation so funny. If we were late on the first issue, it would mess up our schedule for the rest of the year. One thing was for sure, I vowed to myself, the sports section would be on time and letter-perfect!

Chapter Three

That evening at supper my family asked me all about my new job. I told them the high spots, what my responsibilities were, about my interview with Chip. I didn't mention the argument about the cartoon, or not inviting Lizzy to come along when I asked Chip questions, or practically telling Patsy to buzz off.

"Hey, you'll get to sit in the press box at the game. Think you can find a place for me?" Rick asked.

"Forget it," I said.

"Even if I promise not to bug you? I won't even act like we're related." Rick tilted his head and gave me his pleading puppy dog look, which usually gets to me, but I knew I had to be firm this time.

"If everybody on the *Gaz* had a kid brother sitting in the press box, there wouldn't be room for the staff," I told him.

"Thanks for nothing," Rick sighed. "I'm going to stop bragging to all my friends about you."

"My job isn't just fun, you know, Rick. Like tonight, I have to call up the cheerleader captain, Colette Brown, and arrange to meet the whole squad so I can do a story on them."

"That doesn't sound like work to me," Rick commented, and both my parents laughed.

"I don't think anybody takes me seriously," I muttered.

"Of course we do," my father said. "And you know how proud we are. Even your brother John was impressed enough to call home 'not collect' when he heard the news."

"That's true," I admitted. John had called just to congratulate me the day he received my letter.

"You don't have to do all the stories yourself, do you?" Rick wanted to know.

" 'Course not," I answered, but I didn't let on that personally I thought I could probably do them better than anyone else.

Then my mother, whom I've often suspected of having ESP, said, "You know, the best administrators are the ones who aren't afraid to delegate authority."

"I know that," I agreed.

"Especially when it comes to doing dishes," Rick piped up.

Even I had to laugh at that, but I couldn't shed my seriousness for long. As soon as I finished helping in the kitchen, I rushed upstairs to call Colette. I was just about to dial her number when Robin called. I could tell immediately from her voice that she had some special news.

"He called," she gasped, and I knew exactly who she was talking about. Ever since the spring concert, she admitted having a crush on the bass soloist, Donald Carpenter.

Robin started to go into detail about how Donald had broken up with his girlfriend over the summer and now was interested in her.

"Oh, Robin, that's great," I said, "but can I call you back later? I've got to call Colette about lining up the cheerleaders for a group interview. There are eight of them, and it won't be easy to find a time that we can all get together."

"You mean you don't want to hear about how Donald slipped me a note in study hall and—"

"Sure I do," I interrupted, "but this is kind of important. I've got all these calls to make. I mean, if Colette isn't willing to phone them tonight, then I'll have to."

"You mean it can't wait until tomorrow when you see them in school?"

"Robin, the deadline on the first issue is

really tight, and I don't want to waste a second if I can help it. I'll call you as soon as I can, O.K.?''

"Never mind. It'll be too late then." I knew she was disappointed, but I had my work to do. Robin's love life wasn't going to face a deadline, but my stories were.

I spent the next couple of hours on the phone. Colette, who looks like a pixie but acts like a princess, refused to make any calls herself but did give me each cheerleader's phone number.

I spoke to every one of them and suggested they write up a brief biography that I might use in my article. By the time I was finished I was too tired to do my homework, but I had study hall second period, and for once in my life I decided I would use it for studying.

As I was falling to sleep, I worried about whether I'd made it clear to the cheerleaders that I wanted their bios right away. I'd have to find the girls tomorrow and make sure they understood that I needed them no later than the following Monday.

Since the cheerleaders were not all in the same grade, I had to wait until lunchtime the following day to corner them. I always have lunch with Robin and Mary and Sal—whoever gets a table first saves three seats for the others. But I was so busy tracking down the cheerleaders, I barely had time to sit down. When there were only ten minutes of lunch period left and I had managed to see all but one girl, I grabbed a yogurt and joined my friends.

"You looked like you were on roller skates, whipping around the cafeteria just now," Sal observed. Sal, a small dark-haired girl who wears wire-rimmed glasses that magnify her already large blue eyes, is my most outspoken friend.

I explained what I had to do, and that the cafeteria was the best place to find the cheerleaders all in one place.

"How about when they're practicing?" Mary asked. Mary is a strawberry blond—quiet, intelligent, and very calm.

"That's not till tomorrow, and I didn't want to waste time."

"I thought you called them last night." Robin looked at me suspiciously.

"I did, but I forget to give them the deadline."

"You make it sound like it's some kind of emergency," Sal observed.

"Well, it *is* important."

The bell rang then, and I bolted down what was left of my yogurt.

"If you're not careful, this job is going to wind up giving you an ulcer," Sal remarked as she stood up, picked up her tray, and carried it to the rack.

Mary followed with her tray, and for a moment Robin and I were left alone at the table.

"Well, aren't you going to ask me?" She looked at me expectantly.

"About what?" I was still thinking about how I'd handle the cheerleaders' story.

"Betsey, are you kidding? You haven't forgotten already about who called me, have you?"

"Oh, yes—I mean, no," I stammered, although it *had* completely slipped my mind. "Donald called you. Did he ask you out?"

"Yep. He wants me to go to the Kickoff Prom after the game on Saturday."

"You're so lucky," I said wistfully, "that you like somebody who likes you back."

"You've had a zillion chances to fall in love," Robin pointed out. "You just haven't found the right guy."

"And now I'm too busy to worry about that." At that moment, I saw the one cheerleader I hadn't snagged before and, mumbling something about "duty calling," I took off like a shot, leaving Robin alone.

During classes I did my best not to think about the stories I had to write, but the minute the final bell rang, I hurried to the *Gaz* office, settled down at my desk, and jotted down some ideas. I was planning the lead paragraph in my head when Steve Robbins, a roving reporter, slipped a manuscript under my nose.

"This is a story on the middle-school volleyball game," he said.

"Who told you to do it?" I asked, immediately feeling threatened.

"Adam asked me to cover the game." Steve, a frail-looking junior, always looked nervous and self-conscious. I knew I shouldn't be picking on him, but I couldn't stop.

"Why wasn't I in on it?"

"Gee, Betsey, you weren't editor yet when the story was assigned. And to tell the truth, I wasn't that crazy about doing it, but nobody else was interested. The game was scheduled at eight-thirty last Saturday morning, and I was the only one willing to get up at that uncivilized hour to see a bunch of middle-schoolers slapping a ball around." He laughed nervously.

"I hope that didn't prevent you from doing a good job."

"Betsey, you know I always do a good job." His voice was shaking as he said it. Then he walked away. Even I was surprised at how awful I'd acted. I'd always liked Steve's writing, and he knew it. But I had to make sure everyone respected my authority, didn't I?

I began reading the manuscript and changing things I knew were okay the way they were, but again I couldn't seem to control myself. I was halfway through it when someone banged on my desk to get my attention. When I looked up, Adam and Eric Wilson were hovering over me. I don't think I'd ever exchanged two words with Eric before that, even though we've been in lots of classes together. He always seemed standoffish, a loner. I knew that he was considered the best artist in the school. His work was exhibited in every art show, and a collage, which won first prize when he was only a tenth-grader, was on permanent display in the library. I couldn't imagine what he was doing in the *Gaz* office.

I was stunned when Adam announced that Eric was going to be the sports photographer. I couldn't believe my ears, and apparently Eric was just as surprised as I was to find out that he would be assisting me. I soon discovered that he'd been persuaded to work on the paper by Mr. Greely, our college adviser, who thought Eric needed at least one extracurricular activity on his record when he applied to colleges.

"When Greely picked up the fact that I sometimes take photographs of what I want to paint, he suggested I take a job on the *Gaz* as a photographer," Eric explained. "I thought I might wind up taking candid shots around school. Sports was the last thing I expected to be doing."

I couldn't understand why he didn't join something else. "Don't you think you'd be better suited for the chess club?" I asked.

He looked me right in the eye and said in a very serious voice, "Oh, no, Betsey, I couldn't do that. I'm much too tall for chess."

What was that supposed to mean? Was Eric

the Lone Artist trying to make a joke? All right, I'd play along. "How about the computer club then?" I asked.

"Too short for that," he answered, shaking his head and grinning at me.

That grin was my downfall. I cracked up and thought for a minute that everything was going to be all right. But it soon became clear that Eric didn't like sports and knew hardly anything about them, especially football.

All the time we were arguing about sports, though, I found myself noticing how good-looking he was. It was if I was seeing him for the first time. It was hard to keep up my pose of "tough editor" when just looking at him made me feel kind of weak, but I knew if I let down my guard for a second I'd turn into mush. So I guess I said some pretty mean things to him and even asked him if he wanted to quit. But he didn't.

I gave him a book on football basics and told him to be at practice after school the next day so he could take pictures of the Steelers. He told me not to worry, he'd memorize the whole book, but I was plenty worried. Why did they have to give me a sports photographer who hated sports? And why did I feel so attracted to a boy like Eric? Maybe it was just temporary insanity, I hoped.

Just before Eric left, Sara had called me and a couple of other editors over to her desk to show us a revised layout. She was going on about how it was necessary to save space for unexpected news stories and how the layout would not be "permanently fixed" until the last minute, but I was only half-listening. My mind was on Eric, the way he seemed to see right through me. I could still feel the sensation of his fingers touching mine when he took the football book from me. Was it my imagination, or had he purposely let his hand linger against mine longer than necessary? Why was this boy, someone I had nothing in common with, having such a strong effect on me?

He was an artist, and I was a jock. He had never belonged to anything in his life, while I had been a member of Student Government, worked on the *Gaz*, and played on every possible team whenever I could. So why couldn't I stop thinking about him? I couldn't figure it out.

"You do understand, don't you, Betsey?" Sara was saying.

"No," I mumbled, thinking of my own problem.

"It's not that difficult," someone else said, and I realized I'd been daydreaming.

"Oh, sure," I bluffed. "I was thinking of something else."

"Okay, then," Sara finished. "Just remember that you have to be flexible."

I wasn't at all sure what she was talking about, but I was certain I'd find out soon enough. Now was not the time to ask her to repeat what everyone else had understood so quickly. Of course, everyone else had been listening.

All the way home I tried not to think about Eric. We'd gone to the same school and been in the same grade for more than ten years without acknowledging each other's existence, and now suddenly we had been thrown together. Why now, when I was trying so hard to do a good job as sports editor? He could ruin everything if his pictures weren't as good as my stories. And besides, I felt so nervous remembering the way he had looked at me. Had he felt something, too? Did I want him to? But he wasn't even my type! I must have imagined the whole thing.

Forget him, forget him, forget him, I told myself as I opened the door to our house. But less than an hour later, when we were sitting down at the dining room table and my mother had finished dishing out her famous beef stew with wine sauce, Rick brought him up.

"I hear you've got your very own photographer," Rick said with brotherly pride.

"Your very own?" my father teased. "I never heard of owning a photographer."

"I don't own him," I said edgily. "And I could live without him."

"Why?" Rick asked. "I thought you'd be happy about it."

"If you knew who he was, Rick, you wouldn't be saying that."

"I do know. He's Eric Wilson."

"Bad news travels fast, I guess. Who told you?"

"He told somebody, who told somebody's brother, who told me. Anyhow, what's wrong with him?"

"Nothing . . . everything," I said, trying not to choke on a piece of bread.

"I know he's a terrific artist," my mother said. "I remember his work at the art show."

"Yes, but he doesn't know a thing about sports, and he doesn't even like them. I just hope he's a better photographer than he is an athlete."

"You make him sound like a weirdo," Rick surmised.

"I wouldn't go that far," I protested. "Let's just say he's interesting."

Chapter Four

I got up at my usual time, six-thirty, the next morning so that I could run at least thirty minutes, take a shower, eat breakfast, and walk to school. When I got there, I saw a small crowd gathered near the entrance. It thinned out when the first bell rang, and I could see that someone was on crutches. I've got as much morbid curiosity as anyone else, so I walked faster to see who it was.

As I approached the object of all this attention, my heart momentarily stopped beating because I could see that it was Eric, awkwardly balancing himself on one foot. I couldn't believe it. I had spent every waking hour since our encounter the day before trying not to think about him. But Rick had made him the main topic of conversation at dinner, and after that I couldn't get him out of my head. On the way to school, I had decided I would avoid Eric all day, until I had to see him at practice. And now here he was. *Wait a minute.* My brain was switching gears. What was my sports photographer doing on crutches? Was he going to fink out of the photo session now?

I ran up to ask him, but he looked so miserable that I made a few jokes instead, especially when I found out he'd hurt himself tripping in the kitchen. It was just so funny after he'd gone on and on the day before about how dangerous sports were. But he didn't laugh at my jokes. Then I said it was lucky he hadn't hurt his hands, or we would have had to call off the photo session.

"You *will* be there, won't you?" I asked.

He seemed to take my question the wrong way. "Don't worry, I'll be there," he said in a mean voice.

Then I hurried off, but I distinctly heard him call after me, "Later, Boss."

I was so mad I started shaking. How dare he say that to me? I really felt sorry for him, and I'd tried hard to be nice, even though I was starting to worry more and more about whether he'd be any help at all on the paper. *Forget him and do the best you can,* I told myself. If he messed up, Adam would just have to find someone else for the job.

My first class was biology, and I slung into my seat in the back of the room, trying to be invisible. Our teacher has the appropriate name of Mr. Frogg, and the kids affectionately call him Froggy. He's so completely into his subject that it's hard to believe he can survive outside his natural habitat, the classroom. He's one of the oldest teachers in the school— bald, rumpled, and lovable.

He's also unpredictable. Our assignment for that day was on the circulatory system, and I'd come prepared to answer any surprise quizzes Froggy might drop on us—his unsubtle way of making sure we did our homework. But you never know when he'll decide to do something different—show slides, draw cartoonlike diagrams that are much more interesting than the dull illustrations in our textbook, or tell jokes and unusual true stories to make a point.

Once we had settled down and he'd taken attendance, he announced the subject for discussion. "I'm going to talk to you today about a subject dear to your heart—your heart." Everyone groaned. Then, in keeping with his crazy approach to teaching, he quoted a poem he said was written by Sir Walter Scott:

"O! many a shaft at random sent
Finds mark the archer little meant!
And many a word, at random spoken,
May soothe or wound a heart that's broken!"

Froggy usually had a way of making you think he had planned a lesson just for you, but this was too much. I honestly believed he had overheard Eric and me. And yes, my heart had definitely been wounded! He spent the next forty minutes describing the function of the heart, mixing facts about the ventricles and arteries and all those other parts with romantic references to what really happens when you think your heart stands still or skips a beat. "These symptoms," he said, "accompanied by sweaty palms, are often signs of falling in love. But physiologically, all that's happening is an increased heartbeat."

Just before the bell rang, he told us that we might get lovesick, but the disease was never fatal. "As Shakespeare said, 'Men have died from time to time, and worms have eaten them, but not for love.'" The class applauded and then reluctantly drifted out. Froggy had put me in such a good mood that I was hardly thinking about Eric at all.

I had study hall next, and one of the privileges of eleventh- and twelfth-graders is to use the library during that hour, which I decided to do. I wanted to stay busy to keep my mind off Eric, so I was going to research some historical facts about football that I might use as a filler on the sports page. I got a pass from the study hall monitor, then went to the sports section of the library and took a pile of books off the open stacks to an empty table in the corner.

I struck gold with the very first book. There was a listing called *Notable Dates in Football*, beginning with *1916: The Rambling Wrecks of Georgia Tech scored 32 times and crushed Cumberland 220-0. 1928: In a Rose Bowl game, Ray Riegels, center for California U, picked up a fumble and ran 64 yards the wrong way.* There were at least half a dozen other facts I wrote down, and I managed to forget all my troubles, at least for a little while.

Then I happened to look up, and all my mixed-up feelings about Eric came flooding back. For there, on the wall directly opposite me, was Eric's collage, the one that had won first prize. Although I had seen it many times before, it really struck me now, because now I found myself trying to imagine Eric creating it—deciding what materials to use, how to place them. It was called *Autumn*, and the glowing earth colors he'd chosen were just right. The more I looked at it, the more I saw in it.

Was Eric like that, too? I'd only seen one side of him—the one that made fun of me—but maybe there was another side. There I was thinking about him again . . . but it was hard not to when I couldn't seem to escape from him, even in the library. There *has* to be another side to him, I thought again. And I started actually looking forward to seeing him at football practice.

But I should have known something would go wrong, no matter how hard I tried. I got to the bleachers ahead of Eric and watched for him out of the corner of my eye. He slowly hobbled along, making his way toward me, and in order not to embarrass him with my staring, I pretended to be totally absorbed watching Coach Darcy warming up the team.

When he sat down next to me, I started right in telling him who the players were and when to shoot. I realized immediately that he had memorized the book I'd given him backwards and forwards, because he understood everything I said. I was amazed at how much he'd learned in such a short time, but I didn't want to make a big deal out of it. I was afraid he'd take it the wrong way and be insulted if I started gushing about how quickly he learned everything.

He looked as if he knew what he was doing with a camera, too, even though at one point he seemed to forget his job and started taking pictures of me! I was so embarrassed, I made him stop right away.

And he kept making smart remarks about football and putting me down for liking it. I hated him when he did stuff like that and I started feeling really depressed. How can you hate someone and be attracted to him at the same time?

When practice was finished, Chip ran over to where we were sitting and started flirting with me. He acted as if Eric weren't even there, and made some comment about seeing me at the Kickoff Prom.

I could see that Eric felt really uncomfortable and was getting ready to leave. Even though we'd just been arguing with each other, I didn't want him to go. I even found myself wondering what it would be like to be with Eric at the dance—which was crazy, since he was on crutches. But out of the blue, I told him to be there. He looked at me as though I had flipped out, and I explained that I wanted him to take pictures at the dance, since all the players and cheerleaders would be in one place at the same time.

He didn't say anything, just turned away and silently moved off. I watched him hobble across the field, the loneliest figure I'd ever seen. I wanted to run after him and say something. But even if I had the courage to catch up with him, what could I say? That I didn't want him to feel left out and rejected, that I wanted to be his friend, that I had spent half the time I'd been in the library gazing at his collage and hoping it might help me understand him?

"What's the matter? Are you afraid he'll fall?" Chip asked.

"Fall?" I repeated, not knowing what he was talking about.

"You've been staring at that guy as though you expected him to be swallowed up by the ground."

"Well, he's not used to crutches," I said, trying to recover my composure.

"Yeah, he does look kind of hopeless. Probably that's the most exercise he's gotten since he learned how to crawl."

"Not everyone has to be a jock, you know."

"Especially not him. I understand he was overpowered by a kitchen stool."

"So what? It's still painful."

"Listen, babe, let's not worry about *him*. Let's think about us." He put his arm around me and bent his head toward mine, but I gently pushed him away so that his lips barely brushed my cheek.

"Not now," I murmured.

"Does that mean, 'Not now, but later'?"

"I don't know what it means," I replied honestly. Here was the most gorgeous guy in the school, and I was resisting him? What was wrong with me?

"You know something, kid, you're a first for me. It's the only time I've had to do more than wiggle my little finger to get a girl to come running." He was smiling when he said this, but I knew he wasn't kidding.

"It's not you, Chip, it's me."

"If you wait for me while I take a shower, I'll drive you home, at least."

"No thanks, Chip, I feel like walking." My

head was so confused that I wanted to be by myself.

"If you say so." Chip looked at me in disbelief. "You *will* allow me to escort you across the field, I hope."

"Of course," I chuckled, and thought how true it was that playing hard-to-get was often a turn-on—although I wasn't playing.

Just before he ducked into the locker room, Chip said, "I hope you'll at least dance with me after the game next Saturday."

"I'll think about it," I teased.

"You know something, Betsey, you're more of a challenge to me than the entire Franklin team." His eyes swept over me approvingly. Then he grinned, blew me a kiss, and disappeared.

I tried to sort out my thoughts as I walked home. I should have been feeling so high, with Chip's obvious interest in me. I wished I could talk myself into feeling the same way about him. Even though he was conceited— maybe with good reason— he did have a sense of humor. If only I could like him! He had all the credentials for being the perfect boyfriend for me. Besides the way he looked—thick, brown, tousled hair, gray eyes, a strong, muscular build—he was also supposed to be a terrific dancer. We shared the same interest in sports, and we could talk about football endlessly. But he didn't make my heart beat faster, or make my knees feel liquid, or give me butterflies in my stomach. That's how Robin had described her condition when she was first attracted to Donald.

Then it struck me—that was exactly the way I felt when I watched Eric limping away from me. But it didn't make sense that I should be even remotely interested in someone like Eric, much less be falling in love with him.

I couldn't help comparing Chip and Eric. If their characteristics were computerized on a dating machine, I'd probably be advised to go out regularly with Chip and to never see Eric again. But I couldn't *wait* to see him again. I was really confused, and I wanted to talk to someone, someone with experience.

Without making a big deal out of it, I decided to ask my mother whether two people who had nothing in common—except the fact that they had nothing in common—could like each other, maybe even fall in love. I've always gotten along great with my mother, and one of the reasons is that she never pries. I'm not the type of girl who confides every detail of her private life, but I do tell my mother a lot more than most of my friends tell their mothers simply because she's a terrific listener, doesn't give lectures, and, well, I just trust her.

I'll never forget one time when I was seven years old, she found me in the middle of the night sitting at my desk tearfully scratching out a letter to the police. The letter was a confession to having stolen a package of lollipops from the supermarket while she was paying for her groceries. At the time, I thought it was easier to admit my crime to the police than to tell my mother. But it didn't take long for me to break down, even though I expected she'd be horrified. To my amazement, she calmly suggested that we pay for the lollipops the next day and that there was no need to punish me—I'd already suffered enough. I think from that moment on, I considered my mother a safety valve, someone I could say almost anything to, if I really needed help.

I waited until after dinner when she was alone in the den, reading the paper. My father was doing the dishes and Rick had disappeared upstairs, so I had her to myself for a few minutes. I wandered into the den and made an excuse of looking for some stamps.

"Do you think it's necessary," I began in a casual way, "to fall in love with someone who has the same interests you do?"

"Not at all, Betts," she replied. "Look at Granny and Gramps. He plays bridge or poker every chance he gets, and Granny hates cards. And she spends all her time worrying about her garden—in the winter planning it, and in the summer working in it. Gramps doesn't know an anemone from a hydrangea, but they get along better than any couple I know."

"That's true," I said. Granny and Gramps

are my mother's parents, and they still hold hands all the time. "But what about somebody younger? I mean, do you think you would have fallen in love with Daddy if he hadn't been an athlete?"

She gave me a knowing look that made me aware of her mind-reading ability, but didn't let on that she knew I was asking about myself. "I don't know. We might not have met if it hadn't been for our mutual interest in sports, but afterwards it was incidental to how we felt about each other. Two people have to have *some* things in common to get along, but usually it's something deeper than whether or not they both like sports or gardening."

"But what if somebody hated sports and made fun of you because you liked them?"

"I admit that could be a serious problem, but maybe that person had a very good reason. If I was attracted to him, I think I'd try to find out why."

Chapter Five

I was grateful for my mother's advice. She'd said exactly what I wanted to hear and gave me the idea that maybe I wasn't totally crazy to want to know Eric better. However, I wasn't sure how I could accomplish that. I attacked my homework, wanting to get it out of the way so that I could put all my mental energy into mapping out a new approach to him. It would be a big step just to have one conversation that didn't end up with one of us going off in a huff.

I polished off my math assignments, then worked on English. It was after ten o'clock before I could reward myself with the luxury of thinking about Eric. My math seemed easy to figure out, compared to him, and I suddenly understood why some girls acted phony in order to get a guy. I knew art was his passion in life, and although I'm not stupid, I admit I don't know much about it, especially modern art. Maybe I should read up on all the exhibitions in town and mention them to him? But that wouldn't work. He'd think I was just trying to impress him, which would be true. I had to find a more subtle way.

I desperately needed to talk to Robin. We hadn't had our usual telephone marathon, and although it was fifteen minutes after the hour she was allowed to use the phone, I decided to risk getting in trouble with her mother. I waited nervously while the phone rang three times before she answered.

"Hi, Rob," I said. "Hope calling at this hour doesn't get you in trouble."

"It's O.K. My parents happen to be out, but I can't stay on too long. What's the matter?" She didn't sound too happy to hear my voice.

"Well, I've got this problem. There's this guy, Eric, who's the sports photographer on the *Gaz*, and—"

"And I suppose he's not working hard enough for you." Her voice was icy.

"It's more complicated than that."

"Look, Betsey, put it on hold till tomorrow. My hair's dripping wet, I just got out of the shower, and I haven't finished my homework."

"Oh, O.K.," I said. "See ya tomorrow."

I was still holding the receiver to my ear when I heard the click of the phone. Robin had never been so cold, but I told myself that maybe I was imagining it. Then I remembered how I'd acted when she called to tell me about Donald asking her out, and how I'd cut her short in the lunchroom in order to catch the last cheerleader. My best friend in the entire world—and I hadn't taken the time to listen to her. I couldn't blame her for being mad, but how could I explain? She simply didn't understand how worried I was about the *Gaz* job. And I hadn't had a chance to tell her that my problem with Eric had to do with love, not work.

The phone call to Robin, which I thought would ease my mind, had only added to my problems. I slowly got ready for bed, and as I curled up under the covers I thought how everything was topsy-turvy: the job on the paper that I'd never dreamed would be mine was turning me into a grind; the first boy I'd ever felt was really special acted as though he hated me; my lifelong friend wasn't there when I needed her. I didn't think I'd ever get to sleep, I had so many worries. The only comforting thought I had was that the next day couldn't be more of a downer.

Things are supposed to look brighter in the morning, but even after I did my jogging, I still felt depressed. I'd read in some magazine that girls from the ages of twelve to seventeen are capable of mood swings that are extreme but perfectly normal. The article said that during a low period it's very important not to become sloppy and give into a bad mood. It said that when you're feeling rotten inside, you should go out of your way to look good on the outside. That's supposed to help your self-image. So even though I felt like a moldy bag of potatoes, there was no reason to look that way.

I took special care in getting dressed—nice corduroy pants instead of jeans, and then I picked out a rust-colored sweater that I saved for special occasions. This was hardly a special occasion, but I'd been told that it was good for my coloring, and more important, it was the closest thing I owned that could be described as an earth tone, something that might appeal to Eric.

On my way to school, I thought I'd find Robin and act as though nothing had happened. And when I saw Eric at the *Gaz* office, I'd kill myself before I said anything that wasn't friendly. *Act really nice and give him a chance to like you,* I told myself.

But things went wrong from the very beginning. Robin seemed to be avoiding me. She didn't bother to wait for me the way she usually did at the school entrance, or talk with me before class. It wasn't easy to pretend nothing had happened if she wouldn't even speak to me!

I got permission to go to the *Gaz* office during study hall. Early in the week Adam had given me a bunch of statistics on the members of the team, including their positions, previous records, height, weight, and personal history. I wanted to have a few lines on all the players, along with their pictures, on file, so I began frantically typing up the material, hoping to get it done before I had to devote all my time to writing stories and editing. I was so involved in what I was doing that I had trouble getting myself together when Eric appeared.

I wasn't prepared for him, and when the first thing he told me was that half the film he'd taken the previous day had been destroyed, I was in a state of shock. Without thinking, I burst out, "Oh, no! I thought you knew what you were doing!" He looked at me as if I'd hit him. I'd done it again—said exactly the wrong thing. But what he said next made me ever madder.

"I do know what I'm doing, Betsey," he said, as though nothing had happened. How could he act so calm when he was ruining everything? He acted as if he didn't even care!

Then he mentioned that there was still one roll he was developing and that he would bring in the prints at the end of the day. He saluted me before he left, which convinced me more than ever that he hated me.

When he left, I went back to my typing, but I had to stop because my eyes filled with tears and the page was a blur. I couldn't remember the last time I'd cried, and I felt like a fool. *He's not worth it*, I told myself as I pulled a tissue out of my bag and blew my nose.

I still had twenty minutes left before my next class, and through sheer will, I pulled myself together and buckled down to work. But even though my tears were under control, I was still unstrung. When I reread what I had written about Michael Sawyer, the defensive tackle, whom I had described as being 11' 5" and weighing 590 pounds, I decided to quit.

I got through my next classes like a zombie, thinking that my problems with Eric seemed worse than ever. And there was no way of knowing how Robin would treat me at lunch. I was hopeful that when we met in the cafeteria, we'd be back on an even keel, but as soon as I sat down with her and Mary and Sal, I knew I was going to have problems.

Mary and Sal did most of the talking, while Robin and I treated each other like polite strangers. At one point they got on the subject of clothes, and Sal said that her mother has always been hung up on the color pink, so that everything Sal wore as a little kid, from snowsuits to sunhats, had been in the pink family. "Until I was old enough to assert myself," she added. Sal's father was a psychologist, and sometimes Sal almost sounded like one herself.

"As a result, you wouldn't be caught dead in pink," Mary observed.

"As a result," Sal said, "I love far-out colors, even if they don't suit me. Incidentally, Betsey, you look terrific in that sweater."

"You do," Mary chimed in. "I think you're the only person I know who can wear rust. It makes me look like an old orange, but it brings out all the highlights in your hair."

There was an awkward silence, and I knew Mary and Sal were aware of the frost between Robin and me. Sal, in her charming bulldozer style, looked from one of us to the other and started to say, "Hey, what's with . . ." But Mary, who is the world's greatest diplomat, shook her head slightly and then quickly turned to me.

"How's Eric working out?" she asked.

The question took me totally by surprise, but I managed to hedge. "Too soon to tell."

"Has he taken any pictures yet?" Sal picked up Mary's cue that it wasn't a good idea to ask what was going on with Robin and me. What she didn't know was that she'd touched on a subject that was even more sensitive.

"Yesterday at practice," I told her.

"In spite of his sprained ankle? He must be very dedicated," Mary said.

"Or in love with his editor," Sal laughed.

"I'm not his type," I said as evenly as possible, and felt myself blush right down to my toes.

Fortunately, the bell rang so that I could avoid further questions, and I busied myself with getting my stuff together and carrying my tray to the dump rack.

I couldn't wait to get through my afternoon classes and zip over to the *Gaz*. I'd calmed down since my disastrous encounter with Eric, and if the remaining prints were halfway decent, maybe, just maybe, we could have a civilized conversation. I bumped into Sal on the way. She was going to computer club, and since we both wouldn't be leaving until five, she suggested we walk home together.

"Good idea," I said, even though I knew I'd have to be prepared for a quiz on why Robin and I were acting so weird. "I'll meet you at the entrance."

As it turned out, I was grateful that she was waiting for me when I left the *Gaz* office, because I'd just endured one of the worst ordeals of my life. Sal didn't have to be a psychologist's daughter to know something was very wrong.

"You look like you're ready to kick somebody," she exclaimed.

"With good reason," I said.

"What's wrong?" Sal sometimes asks too many questions, but she's basically a good kid.

"Everything," I replied.

"Ventilation, which is a psychological term

for sounding off, is a form of therapy. So why not tell me what happened. Ventilate.''

Sometimes I could kill Sal when she tosses these psychological terms around, but I knew she really wanted to help me.

"I just had this horrendous fight with Sara, the managing editor."

"What about?"

"She wants to use *my* sports pages to wind up straight stories that begin in the front of the paper."

"That doesn't sound so terrible."

"You don't understand. I don't have enough space as it is, and now she's giving me even less."

"You make it sound like a personal attack."

"That's how I feel."

"But Betsey, isn't bickering over space just an ordinary part of working on a newspaper? Shouldn't you just expect things like that to happen and cope with it?"

"That's not all that happened," I grumbled. "Eric took all these pictures of the Steelers—dozens of them—and about three of them turned out. How am I supposed to feel about that?"

"I'm sure he feels worse than you do."

"I doubt it. In fact, I don't think he cares at all. That's what makes me so mad."

"Why don't you give him a chance?" Sal looked at me as though I was Attila the Hun.

"A chance!" I screamed. "That's all I've given him. And he keeps letting me down."

"Letting you down, huh? Gee, that sounds a little personal, Ms. Editor. Just what are you expecting from him?"

"Sal, you're a great friend, but I'm not sure how good a shrink you are."

"Betsey, this is our first session. You'll have to consult me on a regular basis to make any real progress."

I smiled weakly and said I'd give it some thought.

"Betsey, I was teasing! Seriously, though, it sounds like your feelings about Eric are deeper than you let on. Why don't you talk them over with Robin? She *is* your closest friend, right? Look, Mary thinks I'm gross to ask you, but what's going on with you and Robin? You didn't exchange two words at lunch."

"I'm not sure I know," I groaned.

"Maybe you should try calling her. I believe in being up front with my friends, as you might have noticed."

"I tried that last night, and it didn't work."

"Well, tomorrow's the game and everyone should feel better. We're all going to meet at the half, remember? I have a feeling that by then Robin will have gotten over whatever there is to get over."

"Especially if you work on her the way you're working on me."

"Didn't know I was so obvious," Sal chuckled. "Maybe *you* should be the shrink and *I* should be the client."

Then, for the first time in two days, I burst out laughing, and I'm sure Sal thought she had cheered me up. It did feel good to laugh, but after Sal and I went our separate ways, I felt just as rotten as ever.

Chapter Six

I was sitting at my desk, polishing up my first paragraph about the game, but my mind started wandering as I remembered Eric's snide remarks about Chip. He couldn't accept the fact that an athlete could be a hero. I wanted to get my article going before the dance—maybe complete the first draft—but I was unnerved by all that had happened. It was only five o'clock, Saturday, after the game, and it didn't seem possible that one day—and it wasn't over yet—could cause so much tension. The game had been a series of crises for the players, but their problems were nothing compared to the ones I had faced.

I had been uptight even before the game

started, because everyone from the *Gaz* was in the press section at least ten minutes before the clock started—except Eric. I knew he had trouble getting around, but I wished he had taken that into consideration and gotten there early. If he wasn't there to take pictures, my front-page story would be ruined. Besides, I have to admit, I was starting to worry about whether something had happened to him.

My stomach was all tied up in knots when, to my amazement—and everyone else's, judging from the sound of their applause and whoops—this three-legged creature crashed into our section. Eric had raced across the field like a comet. Didn't he realize he could really hurt himself that way?

He plopped down next to me, exhausted. "Gee, Boss, you don't look glad to see me," he said, winking at me.

"I'd have been a lot gladder if you'd gotten here early instead of almost killing yourself out there." As soon as the words were out of my mouth, I was sorry I'd said them.

"Gee, Betsey, I just can't do anything right, can I?" he said, looking wounded.

I wanted to hug him when he looked like that, but my stupid pride wouldn't let me. Instead, I made a joke about how I knew his pictures would come out today because I'd been saying my prayers. He didn't think that was funny, of course. He just took off and started adjusting his camera. I was pretty busy after that, too, but between plays I tried unsuccessfully to see what he was doing. I think he purposely avoided me, and when he did return to our section during the half, I wouldn't look at him.

I was totally absorbed in writing a description of a 43-yard reception down the sidelines by Franklin's tight end, which put them ahead 10-7, when two hands covered my pad and stopped me from writing. My first impulse was to be annoyed, but when I saw it was Robin, I smiled a little. "Hi," I said.

"Hi. It's halftime. Aren't you going to the refreshment stand?"

"Well, I kind of wanted to get down everything about the first half while it was still fresh in my mind, but—"

She didn't let me finish. "That's okay," she said coldly, "I understand. Some things are more important than your friends, right Betsey?" And she turned her back on me and walked away.

I felt worse than ever at that moment. I had been about to tell Robin that I'd join her in a minute, but I couldn't do that now. I'd just wanted her to coax me a little after she'd given me the silent treatment for so long. Then I felt even worse when I saw Eric going off to the refreshment stand with a bunch of the *Gaz* staff, headed by Sara, who seemed to be taking a very personal interest in Eric. Lizzy and Patsy trailed behind the others, and as they passed by me in the front row, they sang under their breath—but loud enough for me to hear—"The cheese stands alone, the cheese stands alone . . ."

I bent my head closer to the pad and scribbled ferociously to show I was so intent on what I was doing that I didn't notice them, but also to hide my face, because despite my best efforts at self-control, a few tears were running down my cheek. After a few minutes, when I was sure they were safely out of sight, I looked up and saw there was no one left in the press section except me. I had never felt so alone before, but I couldn't run over to the refreshment stand now. I just couldn't.

I forced myself to work on my story, but less than ten minutes later, out of the corner of my eye, I saw Lizzy and Patsy, munching on Chipwiches, drift back to the press section. They were all excited, and I couldn't help overhearing them when they sat down just a few rows behind me.

"Doesn't that party sound terrific!" Patsy squealed. "I've never been on a hayride before."

"Fantastic," Lizzy agreed. "It was really nice of Sara to invite us."

"I can't believe it, either. I mean, she's a senior and everything. She did hint, though, that her brother Teddy, who's in my classes, is going, and he more or less asked her to invite me." She giggled self-consciously.

"Well, we both work on the paper, and I

think she's inviting everyone who has anything to do with the *Gaz*."

"Probably. But whatever the reason, I can't wait."

"Me neither."

The bleachers filled up again and their voices faded, but I'd heard more than I wanted to hear. I had this sinking feeling of rejection, even though Sara wasn't a friend of mine. I really am the cheese, I thought miserably, but I couldn't let on how I felt, not to anyone.

A few minutes before the second half began, Eric sat down beside me, probably in the line of duty, and offered me a potato chip the way someone offers a dog a bone. I was starving so I accepted one. I hoped he couldn't tell that I'd been crying.

"So," I asked, putting on a brave smile, "where have you been?"

"Just doing my job, Boss," he said with a grin.

"Eric, I wish you wouldn't call me that. You make me feel like some kind of a slavedriver. Can't you just give me a chance?"

"*Me* give *you* a chance? But . . ." Just then the players came on the field for the second half.

"Let's just do our jobs, okay?" I said. And we didn't say another word for the rest of the game. Luckily, the second half was so exciting that it took my mind off Eric for a while.

When the game ended and we had won, I

was all keyed up and wanted to share my excitement with someone. But Eric didn't even seem to care about Southfield's victory and started making nasty cracks about football again. And we had a fight. A bad one. People were staring at us and making fun. So for a few minutes, we pretended that everything was all right and started walking away. But we hadn't gone far before we started arguing again.

Luckily, we were interrupted when Andy, a friend of Eric's, asked us if we wanted to have a pizza with him and his girlfriend, Jennifer. I knew Eric would worm his way out of it, so before I was forced to suffer a public humiliation, I let them all know that I wasn't interested. Then I jogged home, hoping to clear my head of my whole miserable life.

As soon as I got in the house, I called a quick hello to my parents, told them I had to type up my notes about the game, and ran upstairs to my room. Luckily, Rick was already entertaining them with details of the game, so they didn't miss me.

Under normal circumstances, I love adding to Rick's version of whatever sports event we have seen together, and even he admits that I must have super vision because I've always seen things he didn't. But I wasn't in the mood to entertain, even though I was guaranteed flattering remarks from my father, who is convinced that most sports reporters either just tick off facts about games as though they're describing phone book entries or care more about impressing fans with their way with words instead of describing the game.

"You've got a special talent for writing sports stories," he told me when I was in third grade and wrote a composition on how I caught my first fish. It was a baby sunfish and had to be thrown back, but according to my father my composition deserved the title of *The Young Girl and the Lake*. It took years before I realized that the title was a take-off on Hemingway's *The Old Man and the Sea*, and he was teasing me. Maybe that's why I've always been reluctant to show him my poetry or fiction—I couldn't stand to have anybody make fun of it.

Anyway, all I wanted to do that afternoon was crawl under my covers and cry, but I managed to drag myself to the typewriter. After a while, I just sat there. I stared at my unfinished article on the game. At the rate I was going, I'd never find time again to do the kind of writing I really loved. Then something clicked in my dense brain, and I understood for a moment how Eric felt about the *Gaz*. He wanted to do a good job, I'm sure, but there were other things much more important to him. And the *Gaz* kept him away from those things. Maybe that was part of the reason why he resented me so much, as though it was my fault.

There I was, thinking about him again. It

didn't make sense. He made me miserable every time I saw him, and I had just literally run away from him. Yet I was already feeling sorry for him. Why did I like him so much when he wasn't around? Was there some kind of chemistry between us that caused us to repel each other whenever we were physically close? Maybe we'd be good pen pals. If we didn't have to see each other, we might get along!

What a crazy idea, I thought. Then I heard the phone ring, and seconds later Rick crashed into my room. "It's for you," he exploded, his face beaming.

"Who is it? You look like the White House is on the line."

"Much better," he gasped "It's Chip! Chip Hopkins!"

"Oh, him," I said, disappointed. A part of me had hoped against hope that it was Eric. If we couldn't be pen pals, maybe we could get something going on the telephone.

"Hurry up," Rick shrieked. "If you don't want to talk to him, I will."

"Okay, okay," I said, and went to the phone corner upstairs.

Rick was watching me from the doorway, expecting me to make a face the way I usually do when I have an important call. But I knew this meant more to him than it did to me, so I let him listen in.

"Hi ya, kid. Howja think I did today?" was Chip's opener.

"Decent," I answered.

"Decent?" he repeated. "How about incredible, superb, mind-boggling?"

"That, too," I laughed. I couldn't help myself. He was obnoxious but funny. "As a matter of fact, I was just getting ready to type up wonderful things about you."

"Listen, Bets, I know you'll do a good job, but I think you better leave the adjectives blank and let me fill them in."

"We'll see," I said, thinking he did have a cute sense of humor. Why couldn't I like him romantically?

"I wasn't calling about the article, though. We can discuss that in depth later. Right now I'm tied up with my relatives, and I don't know when I'll be able to break away, so I can't offer to drive you to the dance. But will you let me take you home?"

"We'll see," I said.

"Is that the only answer you can come up with?" he asked. "How about a simple yes?"

"That's too easy," I replied. I wasn't trying to keep him guessing, but there was no way of knowing how I'd feel after the dance. Maybe someone else—maybe Eric?—would want to take me home. *Dream on, Betsey*, my brain said to me.

Chip kept talking. "Do you realize that since I got home I've had seven telephone calls from girls of all ages and shapes, who just want to hear my voice? That one of them *begged* me to send her an autographed picture? What does that do for you?''

''It makes me think we better make sure your picture is on the front page of the *Gaz*.'' I wasn't kidding. That was exactly what I thought.

There was a brief pause, and then I heard Chip chuckling.

''What's so funny?'' I asked.

''I just decided something about you, Betsey.''

''What's that?'' The way things were going all day, I was prepared for the worst.

''I think you're wonderful,'' he said, and then he hung up.

''What did he say?'' Rick asked, as soon as I put down the receiver.

''He thinks I'm wonderful,'' I answered.

''Come on, Betsey, what did he really say?''

''Well, if you don't believe me—''

''I believe you, I believe you. But what did he say about the game?''

''Something about how incredibly mind-boggling he was.''

''Well, he was. What else?''

''Not much.''

''Then why did he call?''

''You won't believe this, either, but he wants to take me home from the dance.''

"He wants to take *you* home from the dance?"

"I knew you wouldn't believe me."

"I'll believe it when I see it."

"You may not be able to."

"Why not? I'll hang around the kitchen or something till he comes in. Then I promise, on my word of honor, I'll disappear."

"I haven't decided yet if I *want* him to take me home."

"You haven't decided? Betsey, have you flipped out totally?"

"I may get a better offer."

"And who could that be? Some nerd who doesn't know a punt from a pass?"

"You never know."

Rick slapped his hand to his head as though he was in pain and stumbled backwards out of the room, muttering.

I sat there, thinking. I puzzled over why, without trying, everything I said to Chip encouraged him, but nothing I said to Eric was ever right. Maybe at the dance things would be different. We'd be on neutral territory—away from the football field and the *Gaz*—and maybe he'd see me in a new light.

I went back to my room and plunked myself down at my desk, trying to type my article. But I didn't get far because my brain was too busy with fantasies about the dance. I saw Eric and me gazing into each other's eyes, both realizing how wrong we'd been, both understanding how opposites can like each other and even fall in love, both happier than we'd ever been. He'd apologize for making fun of me, and I'd admit I'd provoked him. Then, since the gym was noisy and crowded, he'd suggest we go outside and look at the stars. Maybe we'd walk over to the football field and sit on the bleachers. First, he'd hold my hand and talk about how romantic the field was in the moonlight. Then he'd touch my hair and slide his hand gently around my shoulder. We'd look at each other longingly, and I'd tilt back my head, inviting his kiss. "Betsey," he'd whisper softly, bending towards me. "Betsey . . ."

"Betsey, are you deaf?" Rick had burst into my room, and shattered my lovely fantasy.

"No, why, what's going on . . . ?" It took me a few seconds to adjust to the present.

"Supper's ready. I've been calling and calling you from downstairs. I thought maybe you'd fallen asleep."

"No, just dreaming," I sighed.

"Well, hurry up before the spaghetti turns to glue. I don't want you to starve."

"Why this sudden concern?"

"You're going to need all your strength for the dance."

"You know something, Rick? You understand girls a lot better than you think!"

Chapter Seven

As I was getting dressed for the dance, I kept telling myself what a good time I was going to have. But as soon as I got there, I knew it was hopeless. All the ingredients were there—the gym was decorated with red and white streamers, the music was terrific, and the colored lights created a carnival atmosphere. But I knew I couldn't be happy, even if lots of guys asked me to dance. What good is it being popular if the one boy you really care about doesn't care back? I wanted to be with Eric. And I wanted him to want to be with me.

From the minute I walked into gym, I found myself looking around for him. Of course, I knew he wouldn't be on the dance floor, but when I didn't see him at the side of the room either, I had a moment of panic, thinking he might not have come at all. Then I saw him, taking pictures of some of the players, and I had to take several deep breaths to control my sudden lightheadedness. He looked better than ever!

I weaved my way slowly through the crowd, watching him the whole time. He was wearing a black turtleneck, and he looked really sexy in it. When I finally was standing next to him, I surprised myself. *I didn't say anything mean to him*! In fact, I couldn't think of anything to say at all, except, "Hi."

He looked at me and smiled. "Hi, Boss, you're lookin' good tonight."

And I didn't get mad at him! He was teasing me again. But for once it seemed like friendly teasing. Then we both just stood there looking at each other, not saying a word. But it wasn't an uncomfortable silence. In fact, I probably could have stayed there forever if Chip hadn't sidled over and asked me to dance.

I was going to say no, but Eric spoke first. "Go ahead and have a good time, Betsey. I'll take some pictures." And he walked away.

Have a good time? Didn't he know I was having the best time of my life just standing there listening to him breathe? Hadn't he felt the same things I'd been feeling? But I didn't have time to figure it out. I had to dance with Chip.

"You looked like you needed rescuing," Chip murmured into my ear as we swayed to the music.

"From what?" I asked.

"From that camera creep."

"You mean Eric?" I asked indignantly.

"Didn't mean to offend you, babe. I hardly know the guy. Does he mean something to you?"

There was no way I could answer that question, so I said, "I don't think it's fair to attack someone you hardly know."

"Hey," he said, holding me away from him so he could look at me. "Aren't we a little sensitive? You sound like his personal defender."

"How would you like to be here on crutches? I feel sorry for him, that's all."

"I don't think you have to be," Chip said, looking over my shoulder. "He seems to be doing fine."

He danced me around so that I could see Eric, surrounded by the three youngest cheerleaders. They were making a big fuss over him, and obviously he loved every second of it.

"I see what you mean," I sighed, and kept staring at them.

"Betsey, if it'll guarantee me getting your undivided attention, I'll break a leg, too."

"That's not necessary," I laughed, and forced myself to stop looking at Eric and his little giggling fans.

"Good," Chip said. He pressed me close to him and squeezed my hand, but I instinctively held myself back and didn't return the squeeze.

"Are you trying to tell me something, Betsey?"

"What do you mean?" I didn't realize my resistance was so obvious.

"You're a million miles away."

"I was thinking about the interview," I lied. "I only have a few more questions."

He glared at me in disbelief. "This is hardly the time—"

Then, before I could come up with some phony explanation, another member of the team came up and asked me to dance. Chip gave me up without hesitation, and as I moved off with my new partner, I thought that unwittingly I'd answered the question of whether or not Chip would take me home.

Except for a brief time out for refreshments, I danced nonstop that night. I seemed to be really popular with the Steelers. All of them— when they finally got off the subject of themselves—commented on how great I looked in the green angora sweater I was wearing. At least three of them suggested that I go out with them for some fresh air or that we take time out on the balcony. I'm not a prude or anything, but I knew that going up to the balcony was something you did when you wanted more than just a casual friendship, and I didn't want to lead anyone on. And even though I wouldn't have minded getting some fresh air, I didn't want to be out under the stars with anyone but Eric.

But I didn't see much more of Eric that night. I couldn't keep from looking for him along the fringes of the crowd, but when I didn't catch a glimpse of him for the longest time, I decided he must have gone home. No sooner did I make that decision than I saw him coming down the stairs from the balcony. My first thought was that he had probably tried to get away from the crush of the crowd, and I felt sorry for him. Without being rude, I planned to get away from my partner and go to Eric.

I was trying to think of a way to do this gracefully when I felt myself go weak, as though I'd been punched in the stomach. For I realized that Eric had not escaped to the balcony to be alone. He had gone there with Sara! She was waiting for him at the bottom of the stairs, having come down just ahead of him. She looked spectacular in a matching lipstick red sweater and skirt—much more sophisticated than I was in my stupid plaid kilt. If the tackle I was dancing with hadn't been holding me firmly in his muscular arms, I might have fainted. Fortunately, he wasn't aware that I was about to collapse and probably misunderstood why I suddenly leaned on him so heavily as he continued to whisk me around the room.

My partner was the strong, silent type, which gave me time to unravel my thoughts. Just when I had finally decided that Eric and I might possibly have a chance together, I found out he was interested in someone else. And Sara, of all people!

There was no question that they had been together up in the balcony. It might have been my imagination running wild, but I was almost positive I heard Sara thanking Eric "for everything." What had he said or done on the balcony that made her say that? *Will you finally forget him now?* I asked myself. Then I went to see if I could find a ride home. But the only person I knew who was still at the dance was Robin, and I couldn't ask her. She looked happy dancing with Donald, and I was glad for her, in spite of everything. I called my parents from a pay phone and waited outside for them to come pick me up.

I plunged even deeper into my work on the *Gaz* after that. There was a lot to do before the deadline, but also the more involved I became, the less time I'd have to worry about my personal life. I couldn't bear to even think about Eric now that he seemed to be involved with Sara. How in the world was I going to work with him for the rest of the year? One of us was going to have to quit, and it wasn't going to be me! He never wanted the job in the first place.

He brought in his photographs the Monday after the game and created a minor uproar. I stayed glued to my desk while half the staff went wild over the pictures. Although I was dying to see them, I didn't want to give him the satisfaction of showing my interest.

When he finally brought them to me, I was overwhelmed, for there was nothing ordinary about Eric's pictures. The closeups of the players told you so much about what they were really like, and the composition and shadings of the classic action shots could only have been taken by an artist.

I couldn't bring myself to tell him they were incredibly wonderful, which is what I believed. Instead, I told him they weren't bad for a benchwarmer. I instantly regretted calling him a name, which sounded a lot meaner than I meant, but I had too much pride to take it back. Besides, he didn't give me a chance. He grabbed the photos and took off as though he'd been stung by a bee.

It was easy not to get involved with Eric because he hardly spoke to me. But I was dead wrong thinking he'd eventually resign as photographer. In fact, there was a gradual reversal of our roles on the *Gaz*. He became closer and closer to the staff—he practically received a standing ovation the day he appeared without crutches—while I became more and more isolated in my cocoon of work. Work for me was like a bobsled that kept gaining speed while I lost control. It took over everything, but my only way to survive was to hang in.

One afternoon everyone had just left, and only Adam and I were in the office. He was getting ready to leave, but I was still agonizing over a headline for the football story. I had written at least twenty, but none of them satisfied me.

"Time to go, Betsey," Adam said, gathering his things.

"Not till I finish this," I told him.

"You're doing a great job, you know, but I think it's only fair to tell you that a couple of people are upset about your rewrites."

"Why should they be if I improve their copy?"

"It's possible to overedit. That's something new editors have to learn."

"I want my section to be perfect!"

"There's no such thing, and you might as well know that one reporter has asked to be assigned to anything but sports."

"Then I'll just have to write that person's story myself," I said huffily.

"I'm trying to tell you something, Betsey, but you don't get it. If you don't let up, no one will want to work on your section."

"Then I'll do all the stories myself," I said with such finality that Adam sighed and slowly walked out of the room without bothering to say goodbye.

I tried not to dwell too much on Adam's

warning. He'd told me I was doing a great job, and that was the important thing. So what if some reporters couldn't take any criticism? That was their problem, not mine. By the time I got home, I had convinced myself of how right I was.

If anything, I worked even harder as the deadline approached, and my social life got worse and worse. I had less and less time for my friends, and my phone calls were limited to solving *Gaz* problems. I turned down dates, put off bike-riding with my girlfriends, and refused to go to an exhibition tennis match with my family.

Going to the matches was usually a real treat, especially because they took place on a school night. This was the first time in five years that I'd miss them. When I explained that I had too much to do on the paper, my mother looked at me in alarm. We were having dessert and she was dishing out ice cream. With a scoopful poised in mid air, she asked, "Honey, don't you think you're working too hard?"

"No," I snapped. "I have to get everything finished in a week."

"You can still go to the matches, dummy," Rick offered.

"How would you know, *dummy*?" I asked childishly. "You've never worked on a paper."

"You're not the only person on the *Gaz*. Why not take a night off?" my father asked.

"Because I'm the only person who can do certain things," I barked.

"I bet," Rick said doubtfully.

"You bet right," I growled, and got up from the table.

"You don't want any ice cream?" My mother was dumbfounded because that's my favorite dessert.

"I'm not hungry," I said, "and I'll help with the dishes later."

"She's not going to the matches, and she's not eating ice cream. My sister is totally freaked out." Rick shook his head.

Before I was reduced to a screaming match with Rick or a punch in the nose, I slammed out of the room.

"She's really going bananas," I heard Rick say as I bolted up the stairs. But I didn't wait to hear if my parents agreed. I had captions to write, and I wanted to invent a sports crossword puzzle. If I came up with enough good features, I'd knock out the leftovers from the front page news stories that Sara insisted on putting in my sports section.

Wanting to make the puzzle a surprise, I worked on it furiously and had my rough copy ready two days before the deadline. On my way to the *Gaz*, I stopped by the art room to pick up some grid paper for my final copy. I was surprised to hear the sounds of celebration all the way down the hall on my way to the office.

Mr. Loomis was toasting the staff with a bottle of cola when I entered the room. "Congratulations to all of you! The first issue is the toughest, and we're ready to roll! There should be a final reading of the proof, but that's it. The stories have been fitted, headlined, and captioned, and you deserve a party."

"Nice work, guys!" Adam shouted.

I shuffled slowly to my desk and shoved the crossword puzzle in the bottom drawer. Then I forced myself to go through the motions of enjoying the party, although I couldn't wait for everyone to leave. There were some proofs I wanted to read, and since there was only one day left to make final corrections, I was anxious to get started.

When we ran out of cola and cookies, the party broke up. I hung back until everyone had cleared out and then went to my desk to begin proofreading. I had only read a couple of paragraphs when the tears uncontrollably spilled down my face. I tried to figure out why. *I'm tired,* I thought, but I knew that wasn't the reason. And although it was a bummer not getting my puzzle in on time, there was always the next issue. It was life that was getting me down.

Ever since I'd been elected sports editor, things had gone wrong. I needed Robin and she was ticked off at me; Eric, the first boy I really cared about, wasn't interested; Rick, whom I'd always had fun with, was giving me a hard time; my attempt to be the best sports editor the *Gaz* ever had was backfiring, and most of the staff were avoiding me; even my parents didn't understand why I was working so hard. *I can't handle anything,* I thought, and started crying so uncontrollably that I put my head down on my arms to drown out the sound.

I was so miserable that I didn't hear anyone enter the room. Then someone murmured something and handed me a handkerchief. I looked up and saw Eric, who seemed so concerned that I thought my weakened condition must have affected my brain. The next thing I knew, he had pulled up a chair beside me, taken one of my hands and was asking me to tell him what was wrong.

Everything poured out. I told him how great I thought his pictures were. I told him how my job was making me into a crazy person, causing me to fight with everybody, even my best friend, and how being brought up in a family of jocks had its drawbacks, especially when I wanted time to do other kinds of writing, too. I poured out all my feelings. Almost all.

And Eric confided in me, too. He admitted he was partly to blame for some of the trouble we'd been having, and he was gutsy enough to confess that there were times he envied jocks. He talked to me about being an artist and about the personal reasons he was so defensive about sports. When I learned that his father had died of a heart attack before Eric was in kindergarten, and that his mother—who was in all other ways a "great lady"—became unreal about his getting injured, I was ashamed of how intolerant I'd been. I wanted to hug him, and let him know that it didn't matter.

That was when I remembered Sara. But Eric said I was all wrong about Sara, and I believed him, especially when he said something about wanting to get to know me better.

He'd been so considerate of me, persuading me to ease up on my work, listening to my problems, offering solutions. I wanted to help him back. It came to me in a flash that running was one activity he could do that probably wouldn't worry his mother, and it was something we could share.

He put up a feeble resistance when I suggested it, but then agreed to meet me the next morning at the corner of Spruce and Elm—providing I dumped the proofs on somebody else and promised to write a poem.

I loved the idea, and I thought how true it is that opposites attract. Eric must have been thinking the same thing, because when I stood up he pulled me close to him. We kissed long and tenderly, and I clung to him, knowing that Eric, who had caused me such heartache, would help make everything all right.

Chapter Eight

Eric's complaints about running became less and less with each succeeding day. The first morning he was a little worried about his bad leg, but when he found out it wasn't about to fold under him, he began to enjoy himself. By the end of the first week, it was clear that he was a natural—graceful and well coordinated—and he had amazing endurance. He could easily outrun me, and although I originally set the pace, he soon took a wicked delight in outdoing me.

The first time he inched ahead of me, I increased my speed to keep up. But the gap became greater and greater, and I finally cried for mercy.

"Hold up!" I wailed breathlessly.

He stopped and turned slowly around, still jogging in place. "Betsey, I didn't know you were so far behind," he chuckled.

"You might have lost me," I said, gasping for breath.

"Never," he whispered. We were close enough to touch and I fell into his arms.

"Sorry," I said, trying to recover my balance.

"Don't be," Eric said gently. "You can always lean on me."

"I know," I told him, and knew he didn't just mean my stumbling into his arms.

Because of Eric, my life turned around in the next few weeks. He gave me the courage and emotional support to change, to get out of the swamp of work I was immersed in, and most of all to help me admit when I was wrong. He even told me that part of the reason he had teased me so much about my workaholic attitude was because it had reminded him so much of how he had been about his art. He couldn't stand to watch someone else make the same mistakes.

"So you see," he said, "we're really two of a kind."

It wasn't easy for me to relax my control on the paper, but I forced myself to assign some of the important stories to other reporters, to watch my tendency to rewrite, and to take time to talk with the staff. I wasn't sure I could ever warm up to Sara, although I no longer considered her a threat as far as Eric was concerned. Then we had a meeting about future issues of the *Gaz*, and she said she wanted more offbeat items.

"Like what?" several people asked.

"Betsey's piece on historical facts about football is exactly what I mean."

I couldn't believe that Sara had actually gone out of her way to compliment me in front of everyone, so naturally I thawed out. I'd been holding back on showing her the crossword puzzle, but after that I was encouraged. As soon as the meeting was over, I brought it to her.

Her jaw dropped as she read the entries and began filling in the blanks.

"This is terrific!" she cried. "How did you ever do it?"

I just shrugged, as if I made up complicated puzzles every day.

"Hey, everybody," she shouted. "Come see what Betsey's done this time!"

Several kids gathered around, and they all were enthusiastic. Then Adam passed by and dropped a manuscript on my desk. "This is the soccer story that Steve did. He asked my opinion, and it looks very good to me."

"I'm sure I'll like it," I assured him, letting him know that I was no longer going to be so defensive.

"Good."

Every day after that, I found that not being

so hard on myself really paid off. I still worked hard on my stories, but I finally convinced myself that the *Gaz*—and even the sports section—could survive without me. Because I was less driven, the job was a lot more fun, not just a proving ground. Then one day Sara casually wandered over to me while I was standing in line in the cafeteria and invited me to her birthday party. I accepted gladly, although I had a sneaking suspicion that Eric might have put her up to it. It didn't matter, though, because I finally felt accepted for myself.

Things fell into place at home, too, because I no longer felt the constant urgency to get everything out of the way so that I could get to work. I got back on track with Rick by promising him full coverage on his first swim meet. The whole family was in the kitchen helping skewer lamb, onions, and tomatoes for shish kebab when I told Rick I would make the biggest splash possible with his story.

"Doesn't that smack of nepotism?" my father commented.

"Ne-po-tism," Rick pronounced slowly. "That sounds like a disease."

"It is," my mother laughed.

"I don't think I want it," Rick grumbled.

"You don't have to worry," I assured him.

"Well, what is it?" he asked.

"It means people in high office showing favoritism to relatives," I explained.

"In that case, I'll take a double dose."

"Not possible. You see, I won't be writing the story."

"I thought you wrote all the *important* stories." He sounded disappointed.

"Not anymore."

"Mom, I remember what you said about the best administrators being ones who can delegate authority. I'm beginning to see advantages to that."

"I think maybe you learned that the hard way, but I'm glad you learned it," she said.

"You won't miss the tennis matches next time, I hope," my father said.

"That will never happen again." I smiled sheepishly at the memory of my insistence on not going.

"I hope you get somebody good to cover the meet." Rick still was concerned.

"Don't worry, Rick. All our reporters are good." Once I said that, I was surprised to find I actually believed it.

"We'll be ready to sit down in about thirty minutes," my mother said. "You kids can get lost till then."

My father stayed in the kitchen and began fixing the salad, while Rick and I disappeared. I followed Rick, who leapt up the stairs two at a time. I was only halfway up, when he stopped at the top and turned around to face me. Then he came out with one of the few serious statements I'd ever heard him make to me.

"You know something, Betsey, even if the story on the swim meet isn't as good as if you wrote it, it'll be worth it."

"Why?"

"Because when you don't work so hard, you're more fun."

He darted off before I could defend myself, but as I slowly trudged up the rest of the stairs, I knew I had no defense. Rick had put his finger on it—when I didn't work so hard, I was more fun.

I flopped down on my bed and thought how much all my relationships had suffered—especially my friendship with Robin. I missed her terribly, even though I saw her every day. Sal had given up on trying to get us together; Robin was hurt by what she interpreted as my rejection; my pride and stubborness had prevented me from reaching out to her.

But I'm capable of change, I told myself. There was a whole list of people who had recently taken me off their "no fun" list— Eric, Sara, Lizzy, Patsy, Mom and Daddy, and now Rick. If I could only get to Robin without her cutting me off . . . but how? We were never alone at school, I took the risk of having her hang up on me if I phoned, and it would be too awkward to go to her house if she didn't want to see me. I racked my brain to think up another way, and then it hit me. A letter. I'd write her a letter. It would give her time to think, and if she wanted to tear it up, at least I wouldn't be there to see it.

I went to my desk and pulled out a sheet of pale lavender stationery. The letter practically wrote itself, and I hoped that Robin would believe what I was telling her.

I took the letter to school with me the next day so that I could drop it in her mailbox on my way home. It was a roundabout way of getting it to her, but I didn't want to hand it to her or wait for the mails. Robin had rehearsal that day and wouldn't get the letter until after five. She might call anytime after that, and my main problem was to keep busy until she did.

My mother had left a note that she'd taken Rick to the dentist, and my father wasn't home yet, so I had no distractions. I was too nervous to concentrate on my homework, so I decided to make some brownies. I'd just shoved them into the oven when the phone rang. *Please let it be Robin, please let it be Robin,* I whispered like a spell.

"Hello," I croaked.

"Betsey?" It was Robin.

I tried to sound normal, but all that came out was a feeble, "Robin?"

"Your letter's the best thing I ever got." There was a lilt to her voice that I hadn't heard in a long time.

"You mean you forgive me?" I was ecstatic.

"If you forgive me."

"It was my fault. I should have listened to you."

"No, Betsey, I should have understood why you didn't."

"Do you realize how much time we've wasted?"

"I know, but remember we were friends before we were born. That makes up for the month we just missed."

"Not quite, Robin. We couldn't talk then."

"We'll have to have a sleepover, to make up for lost time."

"We'll need at least ten for me to fill you in on everything. So much has happened."

"You're in love?"

"Well . . . how's Donald?"

"Never mind Donald. What do you mean— 'well . . .'? Who is it?"

"Would you believe Eric?"

"Eric the artist, the nonathlete, the misogynist?"

"What's that mean—misogynist?"

"Woman-hater."

"He's not a woman-hater."

"I guess you're the one who should know."

"I do know," I answered, and then we both laughed.

We might have talked forever if my mother and Rick hadn't returned. They walked in the back door, and Rick started sniffing the air like a puppy dog.

"Bets," my mother shouted, "what's burning?"

"Oh, no!" I screamed. "Robin, I'll call you right back."

I grabbed a potholder, opened the oven, and slid out the tray of brownies, which were more black than brown.

"What are they?" Rick asked disgustedly.

"They *were* brownies," I answered.

"They're gross!" he said, making a face.

"I don't think so," I muttered, as I dumped them in the garbage pail. "They're the most beautiful brownies I ever made."

Everything seemed beautiful to me the rest of the night as I floated around in a daze, thinking of how straightening everything out with Eric straightened out everything else, too. Is that what love does? I wanted to give him something special. I'd been haunted by his collage, *Autumn*, ever since that day in the library when I really saw it for the first time. I wanted Eric to see another side of me.

I wrote a poem. It took over two hours to write one stanza. I'd been a secret poet for so long that it took all my nerve to slip it into an envelope with the idea of presenting it to Eric the next day.

We met for our run as usual, on the corner of Spruce and Elm, and I had the poem in my back pocket. The skies were threatening, and I suggested that maybe we should forget about running. But Eric was gung-ho about doing at least half a mile. However, we'd only been out ten minutes when it started to drizzle. We were near a tiny park that had a small pavilion. We ducked in there at my suggestion.

"Afraid you'll shrink?" Eric joked.

"No, but I am afraid we'll slip. You don't want to risk another bout with crutches, do you?"

He grinned. Then he grabbed my hand and pulled me toward a bench in the pavilion. "You look pretty today. What's up?"

"I made up with Robin."

"I knew you would. Someone just had to make the first move."

"I wrote her a letter, and she called right away. We talked forever, and it was as if nothing had ever happened between us. I think if it hadn't been for you, I might never have risked it."

"You had nothing to lose."

"I know that now. Eric, I have something I wrote for you, too. A poem. If you don't like it, I have nothing to lose." I handed him the envelope which he carefully opened.

He read the poem to himself, and then he reread it. "Betsey," he said quietly, "this is beautiful."

"You're not just saying it?"

"I never say anything I don't mean. You know that."

"I guess I do know that by now," I said happily.

"You know what this proves? It's just like I said before. Deep down, we're more alike than you think."

"How about a kiss?" I asked.

"Whatever you say, Boss."

To read Eric's side of this story, flip this book over and begin reading on page 1.

EVERY LOVE STORY HAS TWO SIDES...

ERIC'S STORY

I'm not what you'd call a team player . . . That's why I find it almost impossible to believe that now . . . I am the sports photographer for the Gaz . . .

Eric has always known that he wants to be an artist—and he's never cared much about anything else, especially sports. But after one visit to the guidance counselor, he winds up as the sports photographer for the school newspaper!

It wouldn't be so bad if he didn't have to take orders from Betsey, the *Gaz's* first girl sports editor. He's nicknamed her the "Boss" because she's always telling him what to do and always putting him down—and never giving him any credit. She's definitely not his type.

So why is he trying so hard to impress her—and waiting for a chance to show her how he really feels?

TWO BY TWO ROMANCES™ are designed to show you both sides of each special love story in this series. You get two complete books in one. Read what it's like for a boy to fall in love. Then turn the book over and find out what love means to the girl.

Eric's story begins on page one of this half of CHANGE OF HEART. Does Betsey feel the same way? Flip the book over and read her story to find out.

You'll Want to Read All the Books in the
TWO BY TWO ROMANCE™ Series

Don't Wait to Read all the Books in the
TWO BY TWO ROMANCE™ Series

3

TWO BY TWO
ROMANCE™

Change of Heart

Patricia Aks

WARNER BOOKS

A Warner Communications Company

Two By Two Romance™
is a trademark of Riverview Books, Inc.

WARNER BOOKS EDITION

Copyright © 1983 by Riverview Books, Inc.
All rights reserved.

Warner Books, Inc.,
666 Fifth Avenue,
New York, N.Y. 10103

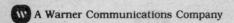 A Warner Communications Company

Printed in the United States of America

First Warner Books Printing: November, 1983

10 9 8 7 6 5 4 3 2 1

Change of Heart

ERIC'S STORY

Chapter One

I'm not what you'd call a team player, not in any sense of the word, and I've managed to stay out of any extracurricular activities ever since I started Southfield High. That's why I find it almost impossible to believe that now that I'm a junior and sixteen years old, I am *the* sports photographer for the *Gaz*, otherwise known as the *Southfield Gazette*, our high school paper.

It's all Mr. Greely's fault. He's our college guidance counselor and resident shrink, and until this year I've never needed his help. I didn't even want to have a college conference with him, even though every junior planning to go to college is supposed to.

The only school I ever wanted to go to was RISD—Rhode Island School of Design—so I didn't need a conference. My grades were good enough, but what was really going to get me into RISD was my artwork, and I didn't need Mr. Greely for that. I've been working really hard for years to make sure I have enough work to show the admissions council that I'm good enough. And I think I am. I'm not bragging when I say that. An artist, just like an athlete, has to know his own worth.

I even won the art prize last year for a collage I created out of acrylic paint, newspaper, ink, twigs, leaves, foil, and marble dust. I called it *Autumn* because it makes you think of all those feelings you get in September when the summer is over. The fact that I was only a tenth-grader when I won the prize was looked on as some sort of miracle, and I was interviewed for the *Gaz*, complete with a photograph of me in my studio—otherwise known as a spare room, with a north light, in our house on Willow Street—and the headline, A TALK WITH ERIC WILSON, in big type. I think my mother, who's my biggest fan, was more excited than I was at seeing my name in print. "It's about time I got famous, right, Mom?" I teased her as she went on and on about the article.

"Especially since you're approaching senility," she countered. My mother has a dry sense

of humor that almost makes up for the fact that she has always, does now, and will always, tend to overprotect me. I've finally cured her of telling me to be careful every time I leave the house. At least she didn't try to stop me from getting my driver's license. In fact, she actually encouraged me to take driver's ed. I tried hard to overlook the fact that she acted as though I was training to be an astronaut preparing for a mission into space every time I practiced with her, sitting in what she still never fails to call the "death seat."

Amazingly enough, my mother has never put any pressure on me about my "talent," as she calls it, or about getting into college. Her only hang-up is nagging me about staying in one piece—not catching cold and not taking any risks that I might hurt myself. This has been going on for as long as I can remember, and I try to be understanding. You see, my father, whom I only vaguely remember, died when I was four years old. He suffered a fatal heart attack before he was forty years old, which the doctor attributed to the fact that he had had rheumatic fever as a child. I think from that moment on, my mother became slightly unhinged when it came to the subject of health—specifically, my health. Apart from that, she's normal.

Mom is the manager of Wiggins, the local bookstore. The job suits her perfectly because she loves reading and talking about books,

which makes her a super salesperson without even trying. Mr. Wiggins, the owner, is a white-haired old guy who looks about a hundred but tries very hard to be with it. He drops in every day to keep an eye on things, according to him, but according to me, I think he really likes to keep an eye on my mother, who looks a lot younger than most mothers I know. The only giveaway that she's almost forty are a few gray streaks in her straight black hair.

My mother and I get along pretty well, apart from the medical situation. She's not rigid about curfews or phone calls and stuff like that, and she doesn't lay any guilt on me about using the car. Usually, I'm not mouthy with her or anything, but once in a while I can get out of line—like when I tried calling her by her first name, Eve, a couple of weeks ago. We were having dinner.

"Pass the salt, please, Eve," I said, testing.

"Here you are, Mr. Wilson," she shot back, and gave me one of her special looks-that-can-kill. That was all I needed—a much more effective weapon than her blowing up or delivering a lecture on respect.

My mother only talks about my father when I ask direct questions. He was an artist, too, and worked in the same advertising company where my mother got her first job after college as a proofreader. They fell in love, got married, made a down payment on the house where we still live, and had me. She gets this

kind of sad, faraway look in her eyes every time she talks about those years, so I don't bring the subject up too often. Once, when I was younger and dumber, I asked her why she never got married again. I knew she had been introduced to a lot of eligible men, and from time to time some of them hung around a lot. I was a little worried about losing her, I guess. But the men who liked her seemed to like me, too, so it didn't seem like such a bad idea to have a stepfather. She told me, when I asked, that she wasn't interested in getting married, and that was the last time I brought it up.

So it's just been Mom and me all these years. We've both had to rely on each other a lot, and her opinions about most things mean a lot to me. That's why when she was so relaxed about the college scene, I thought I could afford to be, too. And I would have stayed that way if it hadn't been for my friend Andy Fenton.

Andy and I have been friends ever since kindergarten, when one day we had "free time" and I decided to paint his face green. He paid me back by banging my head with a tambourine. There was no blood shed, but our teacher, Miss Cartright, had a fit and made a special point of keeping us apart after that. Naturally, her attitude had the exact opposite effect, and we couldn't wait to get together the minute her back was turned. What she didn't understand was that neither of us was attacking

the other. We were just being creative. I was always painting, even at that age, and Andy's face happened to be available. Andy, on the other hand, was always thinking up new ways to make music, and my head seemed like a new sound possibility. But Miss Cartright didn't understand. As a punishment for our "bad" behavior, I was not allowed to paint during free time, and Andy couldn't use the musical instruments.

Andy and I often wonder about what became of Miss Cartright. She left the school after the first semester and hopefully went into another field. I wonder how she'd feel if she knew we'd stayed good friends, that painting is my thing, and that Andy is probably the best musician in the school. Besides being the assistant to Mr. Harwood, the conductor, he plays the first cello in the school orchestra.

Andy and I are alike in some ways, except that he's a joiner. I could spend weeks holed up in my studio, while Andy is busy rehearsing with the orchestra or messing around in the after-school computer club or working on his tennis strokes—he's on the doubles team.

Andy keeps trying to get me involved in some kind of sport, his argument being that my body will turn to mush if I don't exercise. He knows my mother, and so he appreciates my hang-up about sports, but at least once a year he gets me out on the tennis court to hit some. Last spring, when I either slammed the

ball out of the court or into the net, or whiffed altogether, he finally admitted that I was not improving. "Maybe next year..." he said, not wanting to give up hope.

Obviously, Andy has my best interests at heart, and that's why he was able to talk me into seeing Mr. Greely about college. We were in study hall. Andy had just come from his college conference and said that he actually enjoyed it. Andy wants to go to school in or around New York and hopes he'll be accepted at Juilliard.

"Greely says I have a good chance, but I should hedge my bets. He says I should apply to the Manhattan School of Music and Mannes—both in New York."

"And you're going to?"

"What have I got to lose, besides the admissions fee? You shouldn't stake everything on one roll of the dice, either. Some of these admissions committees are flaky, and you never know why you might be turned down. Greely's advice can't hurt. Besides, he's really a nice guy."

Andy made a lot of sense, and so I signed up for a conference the next day. I went into Greely's office and tried to convince him that I was the exception to the rule, that I didn't have the usual precollege admission panic and wasn't even sure why I was there. Greely, a craggy, rumpled-looking, middle-aged man, smiled and suggested that maybe I should be

7

interviewing him. Then we both laughed, and before the conference was over, I had not only committed myself to applying to three other schools but promised to get involved in an extracurricular activity.

"Not every place wants such singlemindedness as you've demonstrated," Greely explained. "And since you say you're interested in photography, why don't you offer your talents to the *Gaz*. Loomis, as you know, is the faculty adviser on the paper, and a good friend of mine. He says the *Gaz* could use a part-time photographer with an original eye."

I had told Greely that I sometimes took pictures, which I used as a basis for my paintings. I'm not quite sure how he got around to interpreting this as an "interest in photography," but I fell for it. Also, he made it sound as though I would be doing the *Gaz* a favor. So I decided to be a good sport and talk to Loomis, who has a reputation for being a crusty character but is also the best teacher in the school. He only teaches senior English, and everyone looks forward to having him. Greely said he was having lunch with Loomis that day and would tell him I'd drop in the *Gaz* office after school and talk to him.

The *Gaz* office is a converted classroom with several desks strategically placed against the walls, a large conference table in the center, and a bunch of chairs scattered around. It was only the first week of school, but the

place was buzzing when I arrived for my meeting with Loomis. Each desk had a sign designating its editor, and Loomis was standing over Adam Winslow's desk at the front of the room working on a master schedule. I knew that Adam had been elected editor-in-chief at the end of last year. I'd gotten to know him a little bit after the "A Talk with Eric Wilson" interview. He was the features editor then and wanted to make sure that I approved the final story. He caught my eye as soon as I entered the room. "Hi, Eric," he greeted me, "you're just the person we're looking for."

Loomis, who had been leaning over Adam's shoulder, straightened up. "Eric Wilson, I presume. Welcome aboard." I shook his hand.

"Er . . . ah . . . hello," I managed to say. Between Adam and Loomis, there was no question that I would take the job. They acted as if I'd already accepted it, and I would have felt like a fink if I tried to get out of it.

"Things are in their usual chaotic state, but Adam will show you around while I finish coping with the eternal time-space problem," Mr. Loomis said.

"I can wait till things slow down," I volunteered, actually wanting some time to adjust.

"No point in waiting. The only time things slow down is when everyone leaves."

"I'll take you around now." Adam pushed back his chair and stood up. "You can learn

9

how we operate by studying this." He pointed to a large chart hung on the wall behind his desk. It showed when stories, pictures, copy editing, galleys, proofreading, layouts, and paste-ups were due for the first issue.

"Only three weeks."

"I know, you think we'll never make it. We don't think so, either, but then it happens. Loomis says the *Gaz* has never missed a publication date."

"I guess my main concern will be getting the pictures in on time."

"That's crucial, but you'll also be involved in selection, messing around with layouts, enlarging and reducing prints—shooting is only the beginning."

I followed Adam around the room, and he introduced me to the editors and staff members. I knew some of them by sight. They looked surprised to see me there. In general, everyone made me feel welcome, and I even felt a flicker of regret that maybe I'd been missing something all these years. I quickly put that thought out of my mind and asked Adam what my first assignment would be. We were approaching the sports editor's desk and Adam said, "Perfect timing. Betsey Noble, who I'm sure you know, is our newly elected sports editor. She'll tell you."

I knew Betsey—that is, we'd been in the same grade forever—but I'd never really paid much attention to her. The girls I knew tended

to be quieter and more serious. She was poring over a manuscript and didn't notice us until Adam rapped on her desk. She looked up slowly, and her incredible green eyes widened in amazement when Adam informed her that I was joining the staff.

"You, Eric Wilson, the Lone Artist?" she remarked. I couldn't tell if she was being sarcastic, but her smile was warm as sunlight.

"Yeah, me," I replied, trying to match her tone of voice.

"You'll be working together closely," Adam told us.

"Why?" I asked.

"Because right now we need a sports photographer."

"Sports?" I echoed, as though I'd been chosen to photograph rush-hour traffic.

"As a matter of fact, we'd like to list you on the masthead as sports photographer," Adam said. "We already have a roving photographer, but he doesn't have time to cover sports."

"Oh, no," I muttered.

"You're not interested?" Adam raised his eyebrows.

"Oh, sure I am," I said, knowing I was trapped.

"Good. Now I better get back to helping Mr. Loomis with the master schedule. Betsey will tell you everything you need to know."

"Thanks a lot," I said as evenly as possible, wondering what I'd gotten myself into.

11

One conference about college, and I wind up involved in my least favorite thing. It was all Andy's fault—

"Pull up a chair," Betsey said, interrupting my thoughts, "and I'll tell you what has to be done." But first she asked me what I was doing there, and I explained about Greely. Then she started asking me why I didn't try some other activity. I couldn't tell whether she was seriously trying to get rid of me, so I decided to treat her suggestion as a joke. I even made her laugh. Looking back, I can see that was when I first got hooked on Betsey Noble. But I didn't know that then, especially when she got down to business.

"Listen, Eric, we're doing a series of profiles on the members of the football team. I'd like some action shots of each one of the Steelers."

"You mean I have to go to the practices and the games?" I said, sliding myself into the chair I had dragged over to her desk.

"Of course. How else do you expect to get pictures?"

"There must be a way," I sighed.

"Hey, Eric, I get the distinct impression that you don't like football."

"Not much," I said, shrugging my shoulders.

"Basketball, maybe?"

"Well, to be honest, I don't usually make it to the games."

"What about ice hockey?"

"Afraid not."

"Then how in the world can you be any use to me?" Her voice was just this side of shrill.

"You know something, Betsey, I was beginning to wonder about that myself."

Chapter Two

It was almost six o'clock when I got home from school, and my mother was in the kitchen, basting a roast chicken. I couldn't wait to tell her what had happened, confident that she would be sympathetic. But to my surprise, she didn't understand at all.

"I never should have had that college conference," I groaned, "and then none of this would have happened."

"It wasn't a bad idea. I'm sure Mr. Greely knows more about college admissions than we do."

"But me, the sports expert. It's all a bad joke."

"You can't hurt yourself taking pictures."

"Thanks a lot."

"Honestly, Eric, it's wise to expand your horizons."

"Maybe. But I sure didn't expect to plunge feet first into a world of jocks. I don't know a tight end from a quarterback, and scrimmage is something that happens on a battlefield."

My mother laughed and said she'd just gotten home and wanted to change into her jeans. "You can fix the salad dressing while I wash up." She handed me the bottles of oil and vinegar.

"Okay," I said, and pulled a small mixing bowl out of the cabinet. While I carefully poured three parts oil to one part vinegar in the bowl, and added salt, pepper, tarragon, and mustard, I thought again about my first encounter with Betsey. I stirred the ingredients with a wooden spoon, thinking that's just what Betsey and I were like—oil and vinegar . . .

I'm not sure why, but once I saw her shocked reaction to my answers about football, basketball, and hockey, I wanted to shock her even more.

She went on with her questions.

"You may not like being a spectator, but don't you play tennis or anything?"

"Nope. My hand-eye coordination is out of kilter."

"You can swim, I hope."

"Yes, but I can't stand to get my head wet."

"I don't believe it." She glared at me angrily. "Well," she sighed wearily, "I guess I'm stuck with you."

"Maybe you'd like to fire me," I offered, knowing I was being provocative.

"It's not up to me, and besides, we're desperate." Her tone was chillier than ever.

"Thanks a lot."

"Maybe you'd like to quit before you start?" she asked briskly.

"I'm not a quitter," I told her, my temper suddenly rising.

"Terrific," she said sarcastically.

"And besides, I happen to be a very quick study."

"Meaning?"

"Meaning I probably could learn the fundamentals of football overnight."

"That's encouraging. I happen to have just the right book for you. It tells all about the basics of the game, with pictures." She leaned over the side of her desk and her hair—the color of Van Gogh sunflowers—fell over her shoulder as she opened the bottom drawer.

You're beautiful, I said to myself, and for an instant I was afraid that I had spoken aloud, because when she straightened up she was half-smiling.

"What's so funny, Betsey?"

"I just remembered that somebody gave

this to my kid brother, Rick, when he was in third grade, so it's a little beaten up. He memorized every play it describes in less than two weeks.''

"So you think there's hope for me, right?" My hand brushed hers as I reached for the dog-eared paperback, and I was so aware of the electricity between us that I'm not sure what she said next. Something about being able to tackle anything, but I wasn't sure if she was referring to me or to Southfield's team. Before I could ask, Sara, the managing editor, shouted from the opposite end of the room.

"Betsey, we need you over here.''

"Okay," Betsey called back. She stood up, and I pushed back my chair so that she could squeeze by. Then she looked down at me. "Listen, I have to go. Do your homework and be at practice tomorrow after school so you can get to know the plays and the players."

"I'll be there," I agreed, "if I can find the field."

She shook her head in despair, but before she turned away I caught a brief twinkle of amusement in her green eyes . . .

"You're *still* making the dressing, Eric? I left you in this exact position more than ten minutes ago." It was my mother, intruding on the rerun of my first meeting with Betsey.

"Yeah," I said.

"Where's the jar for the dressing?" I asked impatiently, purposely ignoring her remark.

"Where it always is. In the cabinet above the bread box. Eric, I hope your new responsibility on the paper hasn't affected your brain." My mother was grinning, and I relaxed a little. I realized how weird I must seem—taking forever to fix the dressing, not remembering where things were.

"I just have to get used to the idea of working in a group, meeting a deadline, and doing what someone else tells me to do," I explained.

"You mean you have to take orders?"

" 'Fraid so."

"Who's your editor?"

"Betsey Noble." Just saying her name made my cheeks burn. I quickly turned away and reached in the cabinet for the salad dressing jar.

"Unusual for a girl to have that position, isn't it?"

"Yep, and she's only a junior." I was surprised to hear myself saying something good about Betsey.

Just then the phone rang, and my mother picked up the receiver that hung on the wall next to the kitchen door. "He's right here, Andy, and no, you're not interrupting dinner. We won't be eating for at least thirty minutes."

She handed me the receiver as she left the room and closed the door to give me some

privacy. I perched myself on the kitchen stool, which I had dragged over to the phone, and muttered into the mouthpiece, "You've really fixed me, Fenton."

"How?" he asked innocently. "Didn't you like Greely?"

"I like him so much that he got me to apply to three other colleges, including one safety called Slippery Rock."

"That's known as insurance."

"Yeah, but he also arranged for me to work on the *Gaz*."

"That won't kill you. You covering the arts section?"

"I wish."

"What, then?"

"Promise not to fall over?"

"Shoot."

"I am, as of today, the one and only sports photographer on the *Gaz*."

Total silence, followed by loud laughing. Andy couldn't shut up. "Hey, don't blame me."

"Thanks to you, I'm going to be spending all my waking hours mastering the basics of football. I have to take pictures this Saturday, and I literally don't know which end is up."

Andy, trying not to laugh so hard, asked, "Is Betsey Noble your boss?"

"She's the sports editor, if that's what you mean."

"A major breakthrough for the *Gaz*, for

Southfield High, probably for the status of women throughout the world—especially with you at her side."

"Not funny, Andy."

"As a matter of fact, I think she's cute."

"Since when did you pay any attention to girls?"

"Since I took a good look at the girl who sits next to me in orchestra."

"Who is she?"

"Jennifer Cooper. Been in our class forever but I never noticed her before. You see, we're doing the first movement of Shostakovich's First Symphony and she has this solo part. She's got these enormous round eyes and feathery blond hair, and she played her solo perfectly. Since I am Harwood's assistant, I only thought it decent to tell her so."

"And she was eternally grateful."

"Not only that, but we found we had a lot in common."

"Like what?"

"We both have blue eyes."

"Hey, Andy, that's really unusual," I said sarcastically.

"We both want to major in music."

"What else?"

"We both like potato chips dipped in peanut butter."

"Great. I can just see you—two blue-eyed musicians, munching on soggy peanut-butter-

flavored potato chips, walking hand-in-hand into the sunset.''

Then we both cracked up, but when I hung up I sat glued to the kitchen stool, staring into space. There was hope for Andy and Jennifer because they obviously liked the same things. But Betsey and I were exact opposites. We didn't have the same color eyes; she probably cared about art as much as I did about exercise; and *nobody* could share my hunger for marshmallows and grape jelly.

Before I could dwell further on what an unlikely couple we were, the timer on the oven went off and I leaped up, not wanting my mother to catch me daydreaming again. In the process I caught my foot on the leg of the stool and crashed to the floor with a loud thud. My mother burst into the kitchen, looking alarmed.

''Are you O.K.?'' she gasped. ''What happened?''

''I tripped,'' I replied from down on the floor.

I grabbed the hand she had extended to me and stood up. I felt a sharp pain in my left ankle and grimaced.

''Nothing broken, I hope,'' she said worriedly.

''Don't think so. Probably just a sprain.'' I hobbled into the dining room, where I carefully sat in the nearest chair.

''I think you should get it X-rayed. If it's broken, you'll have to get a cast.''

"I didn't hear anything snap," I said, removing my shoe. There was a bump on my ankle that seemed to be growing as I watched.

"I'm driving you to the emergency room of the hospital, Eric," she announced.

"Ma," I began, "it's not serious—"

"You never know, and even if it's just a sprain, you ought to have it taped."

"Okay," I said, giving in, knowing there was no way I could talk her out of her Florence Nightingale role.

"I'll call Irwin Newman and have him arrange everything."

"But he's a chest specialist and that's not where my lungs are located."

My mother did not appreciate my humor and explained that Southfield General was Dr. Newman's hospital, and since we didn't know any orthopedic doctors and since Irwin was a personal friend, he was the logical person to call.

"O.K., O.K.," I said, my resistance going down as the swelling in my ankle went up.

Everything went like clockwork after that. My mother got through to Dr. Newman, who arranged for me to be met at the emergency entrance, where I was pushed in a wheelchair into the X-ray room. My X rays were read by Dr. Wicker—a rugged-looking young doctor who said that nothing was broken.

"You've pulled a ligament, which can be even more painful than a break. I'll tape it for

you, but you should stay off it for at least ten days.''

"You mean he should stay at home with his foot elevated?" my mother asked.

Dr. Wicker chuckled. "That won't be necessary. We have a supply room down the hall—Room 101—where you can rent crutches. No point in buying them, and they come in all sizes.''

"Who's going to teach me how to use them?" I asked.

"No problem. Guys like you don't need lessons—it's like falling out of bed. I suppose you injured yourself playing football or soccer? We get a lot of customers the beginning of the school year, because the kids are out of condition.''

I hesitated a few seconds and considered making up a story that would be a little more sensational than what really happened. But my mother was sitting there, and why should I suddenly care about not being an athlete?

"Would you believe I had an encounter with a kitchen stool and the kitchen stool won?''

"You're kidding.'' He stopped taping my ankle and glanced at me to see if I was serious. "I think that's a first in orthopedic medical history.''

Chapter Three

I went home armed with painkillers. Using the crutches wasn't *quite* as easy as falling out of bed, but I managed to stumble around. My mother was relieved that nothing was broken, but treated me like a guest the rest of the night. Actually, the pain pretty much disappeared soon after the pill wore off, but I didn't argue when she suggested that I take it easy. Besides, I had homework to do, and I was anxious to hit that football book. After all, I'd bragged to Betsey that I was a fast learner.

Immediately after dinner, I hopped my way upstairs, my mother looking on as though I were scaling Mt. Everest. Then she followed with my canvas bag of books, which she

dumped on my bed, and apologized for making such a fuss. But before she left, she couldn't resist cautioning me to be careful getting in and out of the bathtub.

I flopped on the bed, skimmed my history assignment, reviewed the French verbs that I more or less knew, decided to postpone my math homework until breakfast, and dove into the football book. The next couple of hours I devoted to memorizing everything I didn't want to know about football, including some new definitions of cornerback and blitz.

When I finally went to sleep, my head was buzzing with T formations, center snaps, and field goals. The last thing I thought of as I dozed off was that Betsey would be really impressed. I couldn't wait to see her and show off. Maybe I wasn't an athlete, but I had other talents that made up for it.

The next morning, I dressed hurriedly so that I would have time to cope with getting downstairs—going down is a lot harder than going up—finish my homework, and not have to bolt down my breakfast. My mother wanted to know if I felt O.K. when I limited myself to a bowl of cornflakes, and didn't have with it my (usual) eggs and toast and (occasionally) leftover apple pie. I told her I was fine, but the truth was I wasn't exactly looking forward to going to school on crutches. The physical problem didn't bother me, but telling how it happened could be pretty embarrassing.

The first person I saw was Andy. Usually we meet each other at seven minutes to eight on the corner of Willow and Main and walk the four blocks to school together. Under the circumstances, my mother planned to drive me, so we picked him up in the car.

"You were fine when I spoke to you at six o'clock last night," he remarked when he saw me. "Did our conversation throw you?"

"Very funny," I said, and reluctantly told him what had happened.

Andy had the good sense not to razz me about it.

My mother made me promise to call her at Wiggins when I wanted to be picked up.

"It'll be on the late side because I have to go to football practice."

"You *what*?" she shouted.

"Pictures only, remember? I'm not about to try out for the team."

"Oh, Eric," she laughed, "I forgot about the *Gaz* job. Do you think you should go to—"

"Yes," I interrupted, knowing what she was about to say. There was no way I was not going to do the job I'd promised to do for the *Gaz*, and the last thing I wanted was to look like a fink in Betsey's eyes. "I'll get a chance to use that telephoto lens Uncle Willie gave me last Christmas." Uncle Willie is my mother's brother, who's a photography nut.

"That's worth the risk, then," my mother replied, grinning.

We'd arrived at school and Andy scrambled out of the car. He held my crutches as I got out of the backseat. "Thanks for the ride, Mrs. Wilson," Andy said. "I'll try to keep Eric in one piece."

My mother took off, and we made our way to the entrance. Everyone looked at me as though I were an extraterrestrial being who had landed at Southfield High. Soon a small crowd had gathered around me and wanted to know what happened. "I tripped," I answered, wanting to avoid going into details. But someone asked where I had tripped and I couldn't lie. There was an outburst of laughter when everyone heard. Needless to say, I was not enjoying this, and I was happy when the bell rang. I hung back, not wanting to slow up everyone else, or have a million eyes watch me do my balancing act.

I was waiting for the crowd to thin out when I caught Betsey's eye. My heart started racing, but I was sure that had something to do with the general strain I'd been under. When she was less than a foot away from me, she looked me up and down for a full minute. I tried to read her expression—a combination of disbelief, amusement, and disappointment.

"I told you to *read* the book on football, not act out the plays," she said.

She was laughing at me and I couldn't stand

it. She probably thought I was a total jerk. She made a few more jokes and then got to what I knew was her real reason for stopping to talk to me. She really thought I was going to fink out of the photo session. What kind of a guy did she think I was? I told her I'd be there, and she took off, but I couldn't resist adding, "Later, Boss." I don't think she heard, though.

During my classes the rest of the day I couldn't concentrate, which is unusual for me. Usually, I pay attention in classes so I don't have to do much studying at home. That leaves me more time for my art. So in my modern European history class, it was unusual that Mrs. Ransom had to call my name three times before getting my attention. In fact, if Joey—the class clown, who sits behind me— hadn't hit my shoulder, I might never have heard her.

"Eric, you didn't fall on your head, did you?" Mrs. Ransom asked.

"What, Mrs. Ransom?"

She ignored the laughs around the class and went on. "We're discussing Hitler's rise to power, in case you didn't know. Can you tell us the name of the elected German president who appointed Hitler chancellor?"

"Hindenburg," I answered. Whew. That was one fact that had stuck in my head from my previous night's reading.

"What year?"

I took a wild guess, based on the chapter

heading, *1933—Hitler's Rise to Power.* "Nineteen thirty-three."

I lucked out with the right answer, and tried not to show my relief. I could return to my private thoughts, knowing Mrs. Ransom wouldn't call on me again.

My next class was math, but numbers reminded me of football. I never knew that a player's number on the back of his uniform meant anything special. But I now reviewed in my mind that tackles, guards, and centers are 50 to 79, ends 80 through 99, and backs range from 1 through 49. I wondered if I could somehow weave my newfound information into a conversation with Betsey. After what happened that morning, I wanted to impress her more than ever. I couldn't wait for school to be over so that I'd have a chance to try.

Classes never seemed so long, but finally it was time for lunch. I was excused from gym and opted to go to the library, where I took a couple more books on football off the shelves. These went beyond the basics, and I spent the entire period memorizing some pretty sophisticated facts—things that even Betsey might not know. I survived the rest of my afternoon classes until the bell rang, signaling it was officially time to be dismissed.

I waited until everyone had left, and then I made my way as fast as possible to the football field. It was a perfect Indian summer day and there was no need to wear a jacket, but I

was still weighed down with my canvas knapsack, which contained my camera in addition to my books. As I approached the field, I could see Coach Darcy putting the players through a rigorous calisthenics routine. Betsey was sitting on the front row of the bleachers, totally lost in watching the warm-up. She was jotting down notes on a clipboard, when I ungracefully sat down next to her.

I was out of breath from rushing and felt less coordinated than ever as I watched the team, who were now sprinting around the track. "I made it," I breathed heavily.

"Just in time," Betsey said in a businesslike voice. "As each player gets near us, you can photograph him. I'll tell you who they are and what position they play."

I whipped out my camera and prepared to shoot, pleased with myself because I'd remembered to load it the night before.

"That's Jeff Barker, coming around now. Number 83."

"An end," I said casually, and snapped the shutter.

"And just behind him is Bud Fisher. He's num—"

"Number 32. A back," I filled in, and took his picture.

I continued to make it obvious that I knew the significance of the numbers, but Betsey acted as if she couldn't have cared less. When the players trotted around a second time, she

gave me a capsule description of each one. If I hadn't done my cramming in the library, I would have thought she was speaking a foreign language.

"John has the best claws on the team, Peter's specialty unfortunately is lollipops, and Ken is a monster man."

I had a feeling she was testing me, so I translated. "You mean John the receiver has good hands, Peter's passes are easy to intercept, and Ken is a combination linebacker-defensive back who's allowed to roam freely."

"Yeah, that's right," she said, and this time she did look a little impressed. But she didn't admit it. She just went on talking about the coffin corner, the stutter step, a swing pass, and the suicide squad.

"I know the meanings of all those terms," I bragged, and wondered why she cared so much about this stuff.

"Then why do you look so puzzled?"

"Because I don't get you. I can't understand why you enjoy seeing a bunch of guys suited up in pounds of gear trying to knock each other down in a game they're not required to play."

"You just don't understand," she replied hotly. "It's a *team* sport, requiring cooperation, precision, skill."

"But they could really get hurt out there—and what's the point?"

"Look, Eric, you injured yourself in the

31

kitchen. The only place less glamorous would be the bathroom. Personally, I'd rather be taking my chances on a field, outdoors, playing a game."

There were a lot of things I could have said, but I was momentarily dazzled by her eyes, which were more unusual than ever in the late afternoon light, and I remained silent. What a fantastic subject she'd be for a painting. I could see it in my mind's eye—an abstract portrait of soft golds and iridescent greens against a stark white background. If I could only capture this moment on film, later I could do a painting of her. "Yeah, yeah," I mumbled, and changed the focus on my camera so that I could take some close-ups of her.

"You agree with me then?" She must have thought she'd convinced me about the value of contact sports, because her face softened and she broke into a smile.

"No, no," I muttered absentmindedly, too involved in focusing the camera on her to bother explaining.

Her mood changed abruptly. "What are you doing that for? You're supposed to be taking pictures of the players."

"Just one more of you," I pleaded, and continued snapping.

"No," she shouted, and pointed to the field. "Them! Not me!"

She turned her head away so that I had no choice. The team was doing separate drills—

blocking, receiving, kicking. One bunch kept crashing into each other and winding up in a pile of arms and legs.

I switched to my telephoto lens and pointed the camera at that group of maniacs who seemed determined to destroy themselves. "That's your idea of fun?" I growled.

"It's part of the game."

"To knock each other's brains out?" Then I added a piece of information I had read in the library. "Do you know that tests by physicists show that when two professional football players collide at headlong speed, the energy they release could move thirty-three tons one inch?"

"Wow," she remarked tonelessly.

Our conversation after that was reduced to Betsey identifying the players and giving me instructions on who to shoot. "Make sure you get some shots of Chip Hopkins, number 26. He's the quarterback, in case you didn't know, and I'm doing an interview with him."

Even I knew who Chip was. He was considered Southfield's dreamboy—a superstar athlete, who was movie-star handsome. To me he looked like a well-turned-out gorilla in uniform.

It was after five o'clock, and I could see Coach signaling the team that practice was over. The players started drifting off, a few passed by our bench and waved, but Chip made a special point of coming over to where we were sitting. "Hope you got a few good ones of me. Don't forget to use your fast-

action lens on Saturday when we play Franklin. I plan to knock them out of their socks.''

"I'm not sure I have a lens that's fast enough," I said, but I think my sarcasm was lost on him, because he promptly turned to Betsey.

He put his foot on the bench inches from where she was sitting, and leaned toward her. "You'll be at the dance after the game Saturday, won't you?"

"Yes," she answered. "Maybe we can wind up the interview then."

"We'll have more important things to do than that." A slight breeze had developed and a strand of Betsey's hair was blowing across her face. I felt I shouldn't be looking when Chip brushed it away with his apelike paw.

I stuffed my camera in my bag and prepared to leave. I didn't want to see or hear any of this, so I pulled myself up and mumbled something about having to split.

"Take it easy," Chip said, still looking at Betsey.

Betsey glanced at me sideways as I started to leave. "See ya," she said. "And I just remembered—be at the dance on Saturday."

"What for?" I asked.

"It's the Kickoff Prom and you can take pictures of the team, out of uniform."

"But still in action," Chip added, and chuckled at his devastating wit.

I didn't bother to answer and slowly left the

two of them without looking back. It seemed crazy that I, who never was big on dances, should be going to one on crutches. But I knew I'd be there, armed with my camera, and with a perfect excuse for seeing Betsey again.

Chapter Four

The next day, as soon as I arrived at school, I made arrangements to work in the darkroom. I couldn't wait to see the results. I knew Betsey was counting on me, and I needed an excuse to go to the *Gaz* office. Mr. Andrews, the man who is in charge of all extracurricular activities and acts as though his life—and certainly his job—depends on everyone participating in some school activity, was overjoyed when he learned I was working on the paper. The previous year he had called me in to point out that I was the only tenth-grader who did not have an E.C., which is how he refers to extracurricular. I remember telling him that my E.C. was art and that didn't require joining

anything. Then he suggested that I participate in something totally different—from singing in chorus to the chess club—but his advice was lost on me.

When I explained that I had taken pictures of the team practicing, a kind of dry run for what I'd be doing on Saturday, he explained that the *Gaz* staff had priority in using the darkroom, and agreed that I should be allowed to go there during my gym and study periods.

"I'll clear the way," he told me, acting really important.

"Thanks, Mr. Andrews. That'll be great."

"Now tell me, Eric, aren't you glad you're part of a group effort, working for a common cause?"

"Sure," I lied, thinking the only one I seemed to be working for was Betsey, and I wasn't sure how glad that was making me.

When I got to the darkroom, no one was around and I immediately went to work, taking the film out of the canister, putting it on a reel and then into a tank, and pouring in the developer. I could hear the chorus rehearsing in the next room. Mr. Blade, the demanding conductor, begged the basses to sound less like lovesick calves and more like red-blooded young men when they sang the love songs of Brahms. I tuned into the words, and strangely I found myself identifying with them, especially the line, "Iron bars will not keep me

from my love." I thought of the iron bars as the Southfield Steelers, and my love as . . . well, Betsey was hardly my love, more like my downfall, the goddess of the zinger. But I wished I could stop thinking about her. It was a waste of time. She obviously thought I was a nerd. And I was sure she would be unable to resist Chip's apelike charms.

When the timer went off, I hung the negatives on a line with tiny clothespins. Then I started to repeat the process with my second roll of film. I had just taken it out of the canister when there was a knock on the door.

"When are you getting out of there?" It was a young, squeaky, girl's voice.

"Who are you?"

"I'm Bonnie. I'm supposed to have something to show at photography club this afternoon and this is my only chance."

"I'll be here about twenty more minutes and then it's all yours."

"But then the period's over and this is my only free time. Can't you do your stuff later?"

"No, this is for the *Gaz*. The *Gaz* has priority, you know."

"Oh, this is awful," she whined. "I should have done it earlier." I could tell she was on the verge of tears.

"How much do you have to do?"

"I only have three prints to make. It won't take me long," she replied excitedly, and then

she flung open the door, letting the light flood the darkroom.

Instant disaster! I couldn't believe it! My prints ruined—all that work for nothing! I was momentarily stunned as I saw the overexposed film self-destruct. "Oh no, it can't be," I groaned. Then, as the shock wore off, I felt furious and frustrated, and turned toward the door, ready to strangle her with my bare hands.

But she looked like a little kid. Her blond hair was pulled back in a ponytail, and her dark eyes were wide with horror. She had her hand clapped over her mouth, probably to hold back a scream, and stood frozen to the spot. I thought if I so much as breathed heavily, she'd break into smithereens.

"It's okay," I assured her, my anger fading away.

"But I ruined your pictures," she whispered. "Aren't you going to kill me?"

"I considered it, Bonnie. They happen to be once-in-a-lifetime shots, never to be recaptured." She looked so unhappy that I tried to turn the whole thing into a joke.

"I know," she said seriously, and her eyes filled with tears.

"Hey, don't cry. They're only pictures. It's not a matter of life or death." I wanted to reassure myself as well as her.

"But you said they're for the *Gaz*."

"That's true. I'll just have to take some

more. Besides, one roll has been saved." I pointed to the negatives I'd hung up to dry.

"What are they—I mean, *were* they?" She tilted her head toward the blank gray film I still was clutching in one hand.

"They were shots of the Steelers at practice. The ones that really count I'll be taking this Saturday at the game. When I develop them, I'll be sure to put a *Beware of Dog* sign on the outside of the door."

That finally made her smile.

"I'm really sorry," she said. "It's all because of this dumb photography club assignment. The president of the club said I had to 'prove myself' and gave me these negatives to print, just to show that I can." She waved the negatives at me.

"There's no reason for both of us to goof up. You still have time to make your prints, so I'll clear out." I took my crutches out of the corner, and started to leave.

"What happened to you?" Bonnie gasped, noticing my problem.

"I tripped a couple of days ago," I explained for the millionth time in less than seventy-two hours.

Her face lit up, and for a second I thought she was going to laugh at me. "Hey, I know who you are. You're Eric Wilson, the Lone Artist."

"Who told you that?" There was only one other person who had ever called me that.

"Rick told me. He's Betsey Noble's brother, and he said that she said there's this guy who doesn't know or care about sports who's been made the sports photographer for the *Gaz*."

"And?"

"And that he tripped in the kitchen, and that she hopes he's a better photographer than athlete."

"And what else?" It was better to know what Betsey thought about me than not to know. Ruining a roll of film was a small price to pay for this information.

"She said you were interesting."

"Interesting," I repeated. "Interesting." No one had ever called me that before. Artistic, smart, funny, but never interesting.

"I think you're neat," Bonnie said, "for not killing me."

"Don't mention it," I said, and hobbled out, a ridiculous smile on my face. I wondered how interesting Betsey would think I was when I told her thirty-six pictures were down the tube.

I still had about twenty minutes before my next class, so I thought I'd spend some time in the library browsing through a new collection of the Impressionists. On the way I passed the *Gaz* office. The door was open, and I heard someone pounding away on the typewriter. I looked in and to my surprise it was Betsey. I hadn't quite prepared my presentation about

the ruined film, but I thought I'd just tell it like it was.

When she heard me thumping my way into the room, she looked up at me and frowned. "I've got to finish this," she said.

"What is it?"

"It's thumbnail sketches of the players. I thought we'd run them with your pictures. I assume you have one of each player."

"Well, I *did*, but you see, there was a slight catastrophe just now in the darkroom. I was opening the canister, and—"

"Don't tell me the film was exposed." She was using her commander-in-chief tone.

"You guessed it."

Then she accused me of not knowing what I was doing, and I told her as calmly as I could that I did. In fact, the more hysterical she became, the calmer I was. One of us had to stay cool.

"What are we going to do?" she screamed. "Here I am working like crazy to do a good job, and now you're telling me there won't be pictures."

"In the first place, there are some pictures. At least there will be when I make prints later."

"Are you sure you can handle it?"

I ignored that remark and went right on talking. "And in the second place, there probably won't be room to include all the players, anyway."

"That's my problem, not yours. And besides, I want to have individual head shots of every member of the team on file."

"O.K., but you don't need them for the first issue. I'm sure there'll be enough to run, what with details of the game, a story on the volleyball team, and the cheerleading feature."

"Thank you for your informed opinion."

"I read the table of contents on Adam's chart, so I know what has to be included. Why are you in such a mad rush?"

She spoke slowly and distinctly, as though I were stupid. "There are forty players, including subs, on the team, and that's at least eighty lines of type. After I write the material, I have to double-check the facts for accuracy, copyedit what I've written, proofread it again after it's set in galleys, worry about the layout and the pictures—*if there are any.*"

"There are other people working on the *Gaz*. There's a copyeditor, a proofreader—and there's me. You have a lot of little helpers."

"Do me a favor, will you? You worry about getting the prints to me on time, and let me worry about the rest."

"Aye, aye," I said, saluted her, and left. I couldn't take the way she was treating me and wanted to let her know it. Why was she doing that stupid job, if it made her so miserable? I thought I'd given her some good advice, but she obviously didn't want to listen to me. As she pointed out, my job was to take pictures

and get them in on time. Period. That's just what I planned to do.

When I returned to the darkroom after lunch, during what was normally my gym period, the negatives were dry and I carefully separated them. It had been centuries since I'd made my own prints, but my Uncle Willie had taught me as a kid and I'd never forgotten. I mumbled the steps àloud, not wanting to skip any or make mistakes: developer, stop bath, fixer, wash, dryer. I timed everything precisely, pleased with myself that I had such a good memory. But when I was finished and pulled the prints out of the dryer, my heart sank. Something was wrong. Except for five or six, they were all too dark. The good ones, in fact, were excellent, but that didn't make me feel any better. Where was Uncle Willie when I needed him the most? And why hadn't I kept up my photography like he wanted me to?

I recalled a piece of advice Willie had given me when I was a little kid and had taken a series of pictures of all the members of our family. None of them had heads! Everyone but me thought that was hilarious. Willie told me then that the only way to become a good photographer was to be totally objective about the finished product, and if something was wrong, to figure out why.

I had until Saturday before I'd be taking more pictures, but I only had a couple of hours before I had to face Betsey. I decided to

closet myself in the darkroom until I came up with a solution. I studied each print, baffled about why there was such an extreme difference in quality between the good and the bad. Then it hit me! I lined them up, reconstructing the sequence, and immediately realized that my first shots were the best. The only thing that had changed was the light. It was late afternoon when I stopped shooting, and I hadn't adjusted the shutter speed. Dumb, dumb, dumb! I was an idiot, but at least I knew it. I heaved a sigh of relief because the mystery was solved, and it wouldn't happen again. I could even laugh about the fact that Chip was a mere shadow—Freud would have something to say about that. I chuckled all the way to my French class.

Our French teacher, Mme. Dubrée, believes that we can never get enough experience speaking French. So after we've completed a written assignment, we have to read it aloud in class. Since she always calls on us alphabetically, I had plenty of time to rehearse what I would say to Betsey. I knew I had to be prepared for a putdown. She wouldn't appreciate that out of seventy-two shots only six were usable. I would admit my stupidity about not adjusting the shutter speed setting, and guarantee her that, barring flood or fire or bubonic plague, my photos of Saturday's game would approach perfection—I hoped.

On the way to the *Gaz*, I planned to head

directly for Betsey's desk, hand her the prints, wait for a mild explosion, and then explain what happened. There were at least a dozen kids buzzing around the office when I got there—all talking at once, typewriters clicking away—and no one noticed me as I slid into the chair behind Betsey's desk. She was totally absorbed in talking to Sara, her back to me, and I hurriedly spread out the prints on her desk. Then, while I waited for her to turn around, I couldn't help hearing their conversation. Only it wasn't a normal conversation— more like an argument. And Betsey's voice was getting louder and louder.

"I have to have more space for my stories," Betsey demanded.

"That's impossible," Sara said calmly. "The front page stories are always tied up on the back page."

"That means cutting the sports articles."

"Can't help it. The lead story is on the Student Council elections. The candidates have to have space to express their views."

"Their views don't have to spill over into my pages."

"I don't have a choice," Sara said impatiently.

"You're purposely making my job impossible."

"That's ridiculous. I voted for you, remember?"

"Probably so you could push me around."

Sara's voice became icy enough to chill a

polar bear in summer. She shrugged her shoulders and said, "There's someone at your desk."

Betsey turned toward me and I waved tentatively. She started to walk over, but not before she got in her usual last word to Sara. "Let's let Adam decide."

I got up from her chair so that she could see the prints, but even upside down she could see the problem. "You've got to be kidding," she said.

"Let me explain," I began. "The reason these are so dark is because I forgot to adjust the . . ."

Her skin had a pink glow, a result of her hassle with Sara—or her disgust with me—I wasn't sure which.

"You're something else," I murmured, unable to take my eyes off her.

"So are you," she said, looking at the prints. "So are you."

Chapter Five

Saturday was a crystal clear Indian summer day, and I knew the bleachers would be filled to capacity. I told my mom I had to be at the game before two o'clock, but she was late getting back from the grocery store, so I barely made it to the press section before kickoff time. And I had to take a shortcut across the field to do it! It gave me a chance to show off my three-legged running ability. I made my way to the press section to the sounds of cheers. You would have thought I was a star player rather than a photographer on crutches. Adam, Mr. Loomis, the reporters, editors—it seemed the entire staff applauded

my entrance, except for Betsey, who looked like she wanted to kill me, as usual.

Everyone else was kidding around, and I had a feeling of belonging that I'd never experienced before. In keeping with the general mood, I clowned around by taking a few bows, and then squeezed into the front row next to Betsey.

I knew she wouldn't accept any excuse for my almost missing the kickoff, so I tried to tease her out of her bad mood. It didn't work. She started putting me down worse than ever, so I just hobbled away to do my job. My camera hung around my neck, and I zeroed in on the kickoff just in time.

I was extra cautious about adjusting the shutter opening, using the right lens, and holding the camera steady. I took several rolls of film before returning to the press section at the half. Betsey was taking pages and pages of notes on a large yellow pad, while everyone else was standing up, stretching, and talking about the game. Franklin was leading 10–7, but the final score could go either way.

"We're getting a hot dog, Eric. Wanna come?" Sara yelled to me from where she was standing several rows back.

"Sure," I answered, and glanced at Betsey, who seemed to be off in her own little world. As I watched her sitting there all alone, I think I started to understand Betsey for the first time—how dedicated she was to doing her

best, even if it turned her into a hermit—and she didn't seem so different from me after all. Actually, she seemed a lot like the old me, before I started working on the paper. It's funny, but the *Gaz* had had opposite effects on us. Now I was more outgoing, and Betsey didn't seem to have a friend in the world.

Then a couple of girls went up to Betsey. I couldn't hear what they were saying, but I saw one of the girls stomp off a few seconds later and leave Betsey sitting there all alone again. I wished there was something I could do to help her, but she'd let me know over and over again that she didn't want any advice from me. What I really wanted to do was go up and put my arms around her, but thought she'd probably attack me if I did.

"Come on, Eric. There won't be anything left," Sara shouted, and I hurried to catch up with the group heading for the refreshment stand.

While we waited in line for our food and drinks, Sara told me about a birthday party her parents were giving her in a couple of weeks.

"We're going to have a hayride, and afterwards a square dance. Hope you'll be danceable by then."

"I'm never danceable," I laughed. "But by then I should be walkable. Anyhow, it sounds great, and I'll be there."

"Don't talk about it, though. I'm not invit-

ing everyone on the *Gaz*—at least not one editor."

"O.K.," I promised, knowing that she was referring to Betsey, and remembering their fight.

When we returned to our seats, Betsey was where we had left her, still writing away. She looked so miserable that I broke down and made one more try to get through to her. I sat down next to her and offered her some potato chips I'd bought. She accepted, but then I made the mistake of calling her "Boss" again, and she got mad at me. I admit I started calling her that to needle her, but lately I had just meant it as a friendly nickname. She'd never believe that though. *Lighten up on the teasing,* I told myself. But by then the second half of the game was starting.

I had to concentrate on reloading the camera and getting psyched for the next shooting session, all the time thinking I wasn't cut out for this. My brief experience as a football spectator had not turned me into a fan. Thanks to Betsey, I at least knew what was going on down there on the field. And it was hard not to get caught up in the general enthusiasm when the Steelers scored a touchdown at the end of the third quarter. But since Chip was responsible—he made a spectacular 35-yard pass that the tight end completed—I managed to restrain myself. When the kicker missed the point after touchdown, I returned to my seat

next to Betsey. But she didn't talk to me for the rest of the game, and I was sure I'd say the wrong thing if I opened my mouth, so I didn't say anything, either.

I'm not sure why everything turned into a contest between us, but that seemed to be the only way we could communicate. I hoped that when the game was over and she had all her notes, she'd relax. This was her first big story, and at the rate she was going she would have the first draft completed before the dance. We didn't have to be in the gym until eight o'clock and that gave her plenty of time.

In the last few minutes of play, although Franklin was behind, they were gaining momentum.

Chip gave Southfield a first down and the game was in the bag. The clock ran out in one minute, and the final score was Southfield 13, Franklin 10.

Chip was the hero of the day, and the cheerleaders broke into a mindless chant that goes "Chip Chip, Hooray! Chip Chip, Hooray!" Then they leaped up and down, waving their pompoms so frantically I thought they might dislocate their shoulders.

"What a waste of energy," I remarked, talking to myself.

"You don't like anything about this, do you?" Betsey had stopped working long enough to join in the cheering.

I was tempted to tell her I liked her, but

something held me back. "It's a good excuse to get some fresh air, I guess."

"Don't you care that we won?"

"I got all choked up when Chip made that run. Such speed, such grace, such power." The minute that slipped out I was sorry and would have given anything to take it back.

Betsey gave me a knowing half-smile, as if she could see right through me. "Maybe if you did something athletic yourself, you wouldn't have to make fun of everyone else who does."

"Maybe if you ever thought about anything else, you could understand my point of view."

"You've been hiding behind a paintbrush all your life."

"You're so attached to your pencil, I'm not sure you could breathe without it."

"I'm doing my job!" she shouted.

."And I'm doing mine!" I shouted back.

What started as a private squabble had developed into a screaming match. And we noticed that we were amusing a small crowd that had gathered around.

"This is as good as the game was," some wise guy quipped.

"Better," someone else answered.

I could see Betsey was dying of embarrassment as much as I was, and I wanted to get us both out of the situation.

"Ready to go?" I asked her in as normal a voice as I could muster, pretending that nothing had happened.

"Ready," she answered, and handed me my crutches.

Then, keeping up the act, we trudged off. We had an armed truce for the benefit of our audience, until they forgot about us. But the minute we were out of earshot, we started up again.

"That was the most embarrassing moment of my life!" she complained.

"Well, you got us into it. At least I got us out of it."

"You think you're some kind of hero?"

"Borderline genius, perhaps. Never thought of myself as a hero."

"You're the most conceited person I ever met."

"It makes me stand out in a crowd."

"I can think of better ways."

We had reached the front of the school, where a lot of kids were milling around. I thought we were on the verge of creating another scene when Andy charged over to us, pulling Jennifer by the hand.

"You guys want to have a pizza with us before the dance?" Andy asked.

I looked at Betsey and steeled myself for one of her putdowns. Sure enough, she didn't disappoint me. "Are you kidding?" She acted as though Andy wanted her to join him in a pile of garbage.

Andy, momentarily speechless, finally asked, "Why not?"

"Don't ask," she said, and then took off without a further word.

"Did I say something wrong?" Andy looked at me in confusion.

"Nothing to do with you," I sighed.

"Maybe she doesn't like pizza," Jennifer suggested.

"Maybe," I said, not wanting to admit that it was me Betsey was running away from.

"Why don't you come with us, anyway?" Andy invited.

"Thanks, but I pigged out at the half." Actually, I always had room for a pizza, but you know what they say about three being a crowd.

"See ya later, then," Andy said.

"Later," I said.

I called my mom and asked her to pick me up. As I waited, I tried to sort out my feelings. Why did I feel rejected in love, when we hadn't even gotten to the like stage? Betsey obviously couldn't stand me—she'd said I was the most conceited person she'd ever met—and the feeling was mutual. So why was I looking forward to seeing her again? I couldn't wait for another chance with her at the dance.

"How was the game?" Mom asked on the way home.

"Cosmic," I answered.

She laughed, knowing my views on spectator sports. "Did you win?"

"Southfield 13, Franklin 10. I understand it was a very good game."

"I'm glad you won. That means the dance will be more fun."

"Yep," I said, knowing that had nothing to do with my having a good time.

I've never thought much about how I looked. But since I had so much time to kill before the dance, I decided to wash up and change my shirt. My Aunt Trudy once told me there are very few men who don't look better in turtlenecks, and especially dark-colored ones. My mother had bought me some shirts before school began, and I picked out a brand-new black turtleneck. I pulled it over my head and then looked at myself in the full-length mirror on the inside of the closet door. My jeans looked a little grubby, so I changed into a freshly pressed pair of chinos. Then I went into the bathroom to comb my hair. My mother had suggested for the last three weeks that I get my hair trimmed, but I kept putting her off.

"I'm an artist, and I'm supposed to look shaggy," I argued.

"Shaggy, yes; unkempt, no." But she finally gave up.

Now, as I looked in the mirror and saw that the back of my hair was curling up over my collar, I wished I'd listened to her. *Maybe,* I thought, *if I washed it, it'd look better.* I

whipped off my shirt, filled the sink with water, dunked my head, and poured globs of shampoo over it. Ordinarily I wash my hair in the shower, but my sprained ankle made that tricky, and I hadn't mastered the sink system. When I tried rinsing, I managed to crack my head against the porcelain at the same time that my eyes were flooded with soapy water. All this while I was balancing myself on one foot.

When I was finally finished, my back hurt, and my eyes stung, but my hair was clean. I rubbed it dry with a towel and then collapsed on the bed. *What am I doing this for?* I asked myself. I couldn't dance, no one was going to take my picture, everyone else would be too busy to even notice me, and Betsey didn't care what I looked like, did she? But I'd gone so far there was no point in changing again. I put my turtleneck back on and raked my hair with a comb.

Then I went downstairs and grabbed two chicken legs and a glass of milk, which I knew would hold me until I made it to the dance, where there'd be enough junk food to feed an army of starving elephants. I perched carefully on the kitchen stool, remembering how my daydreaming about Betsey had led to my fall, how my preoccupation with her at football practice had caused me to forget to change the shutter speed, and how I had gone to so much trouble to look good when I saw her tonight.

Chapter Six

Things were just warming up when I arrived at the gym. There was a five-piece band blasting off at one end of the room, and a humungus table piled high with food at the other. I drifted around aimlessly and tried not to look too bored when one of the players cornered me—he recognized me as the *Gaz* photographer because of the camera slung around my neck—and started bragging about what a great game he'd played.

"I was that safety who intercepted a pass during the second quarter. If it hadn't been for me, Franklin might have scored then."

"Is that right?" I said, proving that I hadn't fallen asleep.

"Do you think you might have a picture of me on that play?"

"Not sure. I took a lot of shots."

"Well, even if you don't use it in the paper, I'd like to have it, maybe have it blown up."

"Sure thing," I said, not having the vaguest idea of what play he was talking about.

Then at least three other Steelers approached me, all with similar requests and all detailing the fantastic plays they'd made. They all seemed to think I was their personal photographer. I was tempted to ask how so many egos could fit into one room, but decided not to waste my sarcasm on them.

The entire time they were bugging me, I was looking over their shoulders and wondering when Betsey would show. It wasn't easy to see around those hulks, so in order to get them to back off, I offered to take their pictures.

"Just some individual head shots," I explained.

That idea worked like magic and momentarily shut them up while they posed for the camera. *Click, click, click,* I went, and then turned away, as though I had some other urgent matters to attend to. The floor was getting crowded and I looked down in order to avoid stabbing anyone's foot with my crutch.

Then I heard someone say, "Hi." I thought

I recognized the voice, but it sounded much too friendly to be Betsey. I looked up slowly, and when our eyes met, I was speechless. She looked beautiful. She was wearing a plaid skirt and a soft green sweater that emphasized her coloring, and I temporarily stopped breathing. I don't remember what I said. I just remember looking at her and wondering why we couldn't get it together. But the moment was broken when Chip appeared behind her, slid his arm around her waist, and whispered huskily, in some stupid accent, "I vant to take you avay from all dis, dahling."

I didn't want to spoil Betsey's fun, so I told her to go ahead. I was sure she wanted to, anyway. I watched as Chip pulled her toward him. The band was playing a slow song, and Chip was holding on to Betsey as though she were his life-support system. *That's the kind of guy she really wants,* I thought. Then Andy and Jennifer glided by within two feet of me. They, too, were locked together and so involved with each other that they were oblivious to anyone else.

I was beginning to feel that everyone in the world was a couple except me. I'd heard of wallflowers, but that always applied to girls who grew on the edges of the dance floor. I wondered if there was a special name for the male of the species—maybe a wallweed. It was hard to believe that less

than an hour before I'd been looking forward to the dance—or more honestly, to seeing Betsey. Obviously, there was no hope for us.

I headed for the refreshment table—I figured that's what wallweeds instinctively do when there's no one paying attention to them—and helped myself to an oversized pretzel. Then I considered my options: I could o.d. on junk food, take more pictures of the players, continue people-watching, or go home. The junk food would make me feel sick, photographing players meant suffering through more tales of glory, people-watching intensified my feeling of being an outsider, so going home—although it was a copout—seemed the best choice. Besides, I had this sudden desire to get back to my studio. I'd been so preoccupied with my job on the *Gaz* that there hadn't been time for me to paint. In frustration, I gnashed my teeth angrily on another pretzel.

I was so involved in my own thoughts that I wasn't aware that I was being watched until the music stopped and I heard giggling nearby. Then I noticed three members of the cheerleading squad, whispering and casting sly glances in my direction. I was obviously the butt of some joke, and once they caught me looking at them, they squealed with delight and came charging over. They were ninth-graders—the youngest girls on the squad and the silliest.

Their rah-rah manner, from what I could see, was a permanent part of their personality, and for once I was in the mood to talk to some girls who didn't seem to have a care in the world.

"What's so funny?" I asked.

"You are!" they answered in unison, and giggled some more.

"Do you mind telling me why?" I was a little afraid of the answer, but I had to ask.

The question seemed to throw them, and they moved a few steps away. They bent their heads in a huddle so that I couldn't hear them, then popped up and surrounded me. They looked like triplets since they were still wearing their cheerleading uniforms—short red skirts and tights, with white jersey pullovers. They must have decided to divide up the answer.

"We never saw anybody act so mad at a pretzel." "We think it's too bad that you can't dance." "'Cuz you're the cutest boy here." With that, they had an uncontrollable laughing fit, and I joined in.

The next thing I knew, one of them gave a signal and they closed in on me again. This time they planted kisses all over my face— one on each cheek and a third on my forehead. Then, delighted with themselves and still giggling hysterically, they melted into the crowd.

It was hard to feel like a wallweed with that

kind of attention. And I had to laugh at myself when I realized how ridiculous I must have looked taking my frustration out on a pretzel. But then I saw Betsey dancing with another jock, and I felt miserable again.

I was just about to head for the door when I saw Sara.

"You look like you lost your last friend," she said.

"Not exactly."

"I guess it's not too much fun to be on crutches at a dance."

"I'm supposed to be taking pictures, but it's not easy with this mob scene."

"I have a terrific idea. Why don't we go up on the balcony. You might get some interesting angles."

"Great," I said, pleased to have a distraction. Betsey wasn't the only girl in the world!

I followed Sara slowly up the stairs that led to the balcony. It was dark up there, and I groped my way toward her and then slumped down next to her in the front row. It was a relief to be away from the wall-to-wall people, but I could see right away that it was not a good spot to take pictures from.

"This is an oasis, but not for photographers."

"I can see what you mean," she said apologetically. "It's too crowded and too dark."

"Do you want to leave?" She had suggested that we go there so that I could take pictures, and it didn't seem fair to keep her from having a good time.

"We just got here," she replied. "It's a good place to enjoy the view."

My eyes had grown accustomed to the darkness, and I could see that several other couples were sitting out the dance. However, they seemed far more interested in each other than they were in what was going on in the gym. Sara was going on about her inability to talk to the Steelers, and I absentmindedly muttered, "You're absolutely right." But all the time I was trying to find Betsey. She was no longer in the corner where I'd last seen her, and I couldn't spot her on the dance floor.

"They're so macho. I wonder if that's one of the requirements for joining the team."

"Probably," I mumbled, only half-listening.

"I prefer sensitive men. You know, the artistic type," she said with a grin.

"Yeah," I said, too absorbed in my search for the remark to register. The dancers were jumping around to a wild punk piece, and I couldn't recognize anyone. They were all a blur, and I was about to give up.

Just then the band changed pace and slowed into a dreamy romantic number. The couples swayed to the music and I was able to see their faces. *Where is she?* I wondered. *And*

why do I care? Then I saw her, encircled in the arms of yet another Steeler. I had all these mixed emotions then—envy, anger, and relief. Envy that I rated zilch on the athletic scale, anger that she only seemed interested in muscle-bound jocks, and relief that she wasn't with Chip.

"Are you looking for someone?" Sara couldn't help noticing that I wasn't paying much attention to her.

"N—no, yes, I mean, I found her," I stuttered. I could feel my face burn with embarrassment and was grateful for the dim light.

Sara burst out laughing. "I don't think you heard one word I said."

"Sure I did. You said you never met an artistic football player."

"Close, but not exactly." She continued laughing.

"What's so funny?" I asked.

"I'm really laughing at myself. You see, I thought I was doing you a favor, flirting with you a little. But it turns out I needed you more than you needed me."

"You needed me?"

"I used you as an excuse to unload my partner. He kept cutting in on me, and for a mad moment I thought it was because he liked me."

"What made you think differently?"

"He was that defensive end who looked

like a one-man steamroller during the game. All he could talk about was his forearm smashes, his stall-and-yank moves, his fakes, his power. Then he hinted strongly that he'd be a terrific person to interview, and since I was the managing editor, maybe I could arrange it.''

"What did you say?''

"I told him that he should ask Adam to dance, since he was the editor-in-chief. And then I mumbled something about having to check something out with the photographer—you—and I made my getaway.''

"I admire your honesty, Sara, and I'm glad I could help you out.''

"I owe you a favor now. So if I can ever pay you back, let me know.''

"You'll be the first.''

"He's probably boring somebody else now, so it'll be safe for me to return to the dance.''

"Let's go,'' I said, thinking I wasn't the only one who had problems.

We edged out of our balcony seats and headed downstairs, with Sara leading the way. She waited for me at the foot of the stairs, and then, because the music was amplified more than ever, she was forced to shout in order to be heard. "Thanks again, Eric, for everything.''

She moved off just as Betsey danced by. Betsey looked at me blankly, and then dreamily floated off in the arms of yet another Steeler.

She'd been so busy all night that she didn't have time for me, and I sadly decided that for me the party was over.

Chapter Seven

On Sunday my mother and I went to visit my aunt and uncle. We spent the day and had an early supper—a ritual that has been going on for years. Truthfully, though, I enjoy it, especially seeing Uncle Willie. He treats me almost as if I were his own son and always takes me aside for a "man-to-man" talk after supper.

I was especially glad I'd be seeing him the day after the dance. His darkroom is as well equipped as Southfield's, and I could develop my film and have the prints ready for Monday. Proof that I took my job seriously, in case anybody—like Betsey—was interested. Also, I was anxious to see if my creative shots,

where I let my camera do its own thing, made any artistic sense.

Willie, after recovering from the shock that I had photographed an entire football game, was just as eager as I was to develop the film. As he helped me set up things in the darkroom, he said he'd never seen me so jumpy. "You act as though your reputation is at stake."

"It is," I told him, and explained how I'd blown the practice film.

"That won't happen now. And you've got such a good eye, your prints are bound to be good."

"Hope so," I said. I knew I was more concerned with Betsey's reaction than anything else.

I meticulously developed the film, and while we waited for the negatives to dry, Willie showed me the home computer Trudy had given him for his birthday. He warned me that video games were addictive and after "booting the diskette"—computer language for placing a bendable record in the computer—with Pac-Man, I was hooked.

A couple of hours later we came up for air. By then the negatives had dried and I was ready to make prints. There were plenty of conventional action shots, but I must have instinctively zeroed in on facial expressions. They revealed more about the players and their reactions—anguish, pain, pleasure, fear, excitement—than any written profile. I knew

the shots were good, but before I got carried away, I wanted Willie's opinion. He's always a severe critic, and never settles for second-best.

Willie helped me spread the prints out on the floor of the family room. He appraised them silently, picked up a few for closer inspection, piled some together, and shuffled through them.

"What's the verdict?" I asked, unable to sweat it out any longer.

"You want my honest opinion, don't you?"

"Of course." I nervously gritted my teeth.

"They're excellent."

"You mean it, Willie?"

"I wouldn't say so if I didn't. The faces are extraordinary. And do you realize how you could crop some of these action shots to show footwork?" He covered the top of a print with his hand so that only a tangle of feet was revealed.

"It does make a crazy pattern."

"Looks like a clodhopper's ballet," he chuckled.

"I can see the caption now—*A Study in Athletes' Feet*," I said.

Then we both laughed so hard that my mother and Trudy rushed in to see what they were missing. "What's going on?" they asked in unison.

Willie handed each of them a small pile of prints which they flipped through, ohhing and

ahhing all the time as only a devoted mother and aunt can do.

I can't deny that I enjoyed being the center of attention, but more than that, I knew for sure that the pictures were winners. I could present them to the *Gaz* with pride.

I couldn't wait until the next day. I'd sorted them out, eliminated the ones that weren't first-rate, and brought the remaining batch to the office as soon as the last bell rang. The place was roaring with activity, which I discovered became more intense and frenetic as closing date approached. When I arrived, Adam was at his desk surrounded by half a dozen people, including Mr. Loomis. They were working on the front page layout—deciding which story had priority—when Sara saw me come in with my photos.

"This might solve it," she announced, pointing to me. "What we need is a strong picture to grab the reader. Let's see what you've got, Eric."

While I handed the prints to Adam, I noticed Betsey was at her desk typing. *No point in asking her to come over*, I thought. *She'll see them soon enough.*

Adam slowly sifted through the prints and then passed them around. "Dynamite," he exclaimed.

"Best we've ever had," Mr. Loomis, who had been looking over Adam's shoulder, observed.

Then the others outdid themselves with compliments, and I couldn't stop smiling.

"The only unfortunate thing is we can only use a few of these now, but we'll definitely run the rest in our end-of-the-year supplement," Loomis said.

Betsey had tuned out what was going on at our end of the room until Adam shouted to her, "Hey, Betsey, can you tear yourself away long enough to look at these pictures?"

"In a minute," she answered.

"I'll bring them over," I volunteered, wanting to be more or less alone when she reacted to them.

I went over to her desk and put the pile of photos in front of her.

"They're terrific," Adam called to her. "So good, in fact, that our problem will be in selecting the best."

Betsey flipped through the prints hurriedly, and I waited, confident of her praise.

"Not bad for a benchwarmer," she remarked. Her voice was dripping with sarcasm, but I wasn't in the mood to match wits. The success of my pictures meant so much to me and I wasn't about to let her spoil it. I vowed then and there to stop wasting my time with her.

Without another word, I picked up the prints, turned my back on her, and as briskly as possible went back to Adam's desk. I got surprisingly involved in discussing layout, learning about typeface, arguing whether cartoons

should be a regular feature of each issue. Betsey kept pounding away at her typewriter, which made it easy for me to avoid her.

Our contact with each other was kept to a minimum for the next ten days. We only spoke when absolutely necessary, always because of some problem on the paper. I checked in at the *Gaz* every day after school, did what was required, talked with everyone except Betsey, and left. It was a form of self-protection, and it seemed to be working. She made it easy with her impersonal, businesslike attitude. Sometimes she was almost too obvious about it— like the day I arrived in the office without crutches and everyone except Betsey let out a cheer.

Then I noticed that it wasn't just me Betsey was avoiding. She was turning into a workaholic, and never stopped editing, rewriting, proofreading, and then repeating the whole process. I couldn't help overhearing Steve Robbins, one of the sports reporters, complaining to Adam that Betsey had reworked his article so many times that he no longer recognized it.

"You're not the first one to tell me that," Adam said. "And I've already told her to lay off on the rewrites. Let me know if she doesn't take the hint."

It was two days before countdown, and miraculously all the stories were in and edited, pictures selected, captions written, layouts finished. There was still time to make corrections

in galleys, but the entire staff was feeling manic, knowing we were on schedule. Mr. Loomis provided us with a case of Coke and a ton of Famous Amos chocolate chip cookies to celebrate our meeting the deadline. At five o'clock, a half hour before the school officially closed, we drifted out.

I was halfway out the building when I realized that I'd left my knapsack on Adam's desk. I trudged back to the *Gaz,* still a little worried about straining my newly healed ligament, and entered the office. I was sure everyone had left for the day so I was surprised to hear a muffled sound coming from the far end of the room. Then I realized it was Betsey, still at her desk, her head buried in her arms on top of a set of proofs, her shoulders heaving up and down. She was crying.

For a second, I thought I'd grab my knapsack and run without her seeing me, but something pulled me toward her. She suddenly seemed so helpless, I had to say something. I quietly moved in her direction.

"Here," I whispered, and shoved a handkerchief at her. "You're getting those proofs waterlogged."

She grasped the handkerchief, raised her head slowly, and, still sniffling, blotted her face. "Thanks," she murmured so softly I could barely hear her.

"What's wrong?" I asked, sitting down next to her and holding her hand. I didn't even

think about what I was doing. I did it because I wanted to.

"Everything," she cried, as the tears welled up in her eyes.

"Tell me," I encouraged her.

"You're one of the reasons," she blurted. "I mean, I really thought your pictures were fabulous, but I couldn't come out and say it, so I made that cruddy remark about you being a benchwarmer. I wouldn't blame you if you didn't forgive me, but I am sorry."

"I'm the forgiving type. Besides, it's partly my fault that we can never say anything civilized to each other. Maybe because . . . we care too much." I almost couldn't believe what I was saying, but she was being so honest, I felt I had to level with her.

"Maybe," she agreed, and smiled. "But there are other things. Like I haven't spoken to my best friend, Robin, in days. We've been friends forever, and we've never had a fight that lasted more than five minutes."

"I bet she's mad at you for spending so much time working on the paper that you don't have time for her." I remembered that scene during the half at the football game when Betsey couldn't tear herself away for a Coke.

"Are you a mind reader?"

"Maybe," I answered. "But I believe that it takes more than one dumb fight to break up a forever friendship."

"That's not all, though. Adam told me the reporters are complaining that I rewrite too much."

"Well, do you?"

"I'm just trying to do a good job, and everybody hates me for it."

"It's possible you're trying too hard."

"This job, which I thought was going to be so great, is making me a wreck. I love writing, other kinds of writing more than straight reporting. There just hasn't been time for anything like that lately. You're lucky, Eric, that you don't care at all about sports or proving yourself."

"Wait a minute, Betsey. First of all, my art is where I prove myself, and if you think that comes easy, you're wrong. Second of all, there have been plenty of times I'd rather be a dumb jock than anything." Then to my amazement, I found myself telling her about my father dying when I was so young and my mother being super-cautious about me getting hurt.

"Now I feel worse than ever that I made fun of you," Betsey said. "You really couldn't change the way you were raised," she sympathized.

"Neither could you," I answered. Then I saw a look of panic cross her face. "What's wrong, Betsey?"

"Oh, Eric, I'm sorry for changing the subject,

but I just remembered something. What about Sara?''

''What about her?'' I asked, puzzled.

''I thought you two were...you know, seeing each other.''

''Sara and I are friends. Period. Now let's talk about you and me. I think we have to get to know each other better. And to do that, I think you've got to stop worrying so much about the paper and let other people—including me—take some of the work off your shoulders. Will you try?''

''I'll try,'' she said, ''if you'll try something for yourself.''

''As long as it's not dangerous to my health,'' I laughed.

''It's not, although it *is* physical.''

''Physical?'' I said, raising my eyebrows.

''It doesn't involve direct contact, it doesn't have to be competitive, and you might actually enjoy it.''

''Eating chocolate?''

''Running,'' she said. ''I do it every morning before school.''

''Well,'' I said uncertainly, ''I'll have to take it easy at first, because of my leg.''

''We'll start out slow with just a couple of turns around the block at Spruce and Elm, tomorrow morning at seven. Deal?''

''Deal,'' I said. ''But now you've got to leave these proofs and stop thinking about the *Gaz*. The next thing you write should be a

poem, or a short story—nothing to do with sports.''

"That's the best assignment you could have given me."

She pushed back her chair and stood up. Her eyes were misty but her smile was beautiful. I pulled her close to me. She didn't say anything, but put her arms around me and pressed her lips against mine.

Chapter Eight

Andy and I had ducked out of school to go to the Pizza Palace for lunch. Between my going to the *Gaz* every day and Andy's rehearsals and computer club meetings—to say nothing of our time-consuming love lives—we decided we needed a place to talk.

"That Betsey's amazing," Andy said, between bites of pizza.

"What do you mean?" He was on my favorite subject and I wanted to hear more.

"She has accomplished in a few weeks what I have been trying to do all my life."

"What's that?"

"She's gotten you into a sport, and you like it!"

"More than like it. I'm hooked."

"You're probably good at it, too."

"Well, I'm not exactly ready for the Boston Marathon, but I'm getting there. How are you and Jennifer getting along?" I asked, to change the subject.

"Great. You know, I've never felt comfortable with a girl before. I always thought they were another species. Jennifer's made me realize that they think and feel almost the same way we do."

"Yeah, I know what you mean. I've been finding out how little I knew about Betsey. Did you know that she actually writes poems?"

"You're kidding."

"Nope. She even wrote one for me. It's called 'Autumn'—it's based on that collage I did, the one that hangs in the library."

"Wow."

"And I could tell when I read it that she really knew what the collage was all about."

"Here's to girls," Andy said, raising his glass of Coke.

"I'll drink to that," I said, raising mine.

One of the best parts about my running was that Betsey and I were together every morning. After we clocked our minimum couple of miles, we'd take a breather on a bench in a small park on our way home. The park was deserted at that early hour and made us feel far away from the world. It had a special meaning

for both of us, because it was there that we really talked and our trust in each other grew.

Sometimes it came as a shock to realize how wrong we'd been about each other. I'd already told her about Sara, so I felt free to ask her about Chip. She said she'd never been attracted to him for a second.

"You're full of surprises, Betsey," I said when I heard that, "and all good ones."

"I think you'll be surprised to know that we have exactly twenty-three minutes to get home, get showered, and get to school." She stood up and tugged at my arm.

"I'll race you," I challenged her as I got to my feet.

"I thought you didn't like competition," she said with a sly smile.

"You've changed all that, Betsey. I just now discovered that it can be a lot of fun."

"Told you so," she said.

"You've been right about a lot of things, including your prediction that even my mother wouldn't be afraid of my running."

"Tell me about it later. We've got to make tracks now."

"I know," I said. "There never seems to be enough time."

"If we're late for school, your mother may change her mind about my influence on you."

"I don't think you have to worry," I said, as the two of us took off.

That night my mother presented me with proof that she was more than pleased with my running. She brought home a jogging suit, which I tried on while she was messing around in the kitchen.

"You really approve, don't you?" I asked, while I tried on the outfit.

"That girl's a genius," she commented, opening a can of mushroom soup.

"Perfect," I told her.

"You mean Betsey?"

"I mean the running." I could feel my face begin to burn. I'd never discussed Betsey with my mother, and she never asked questions. But not talking about her was getting harder and harder, and here was my chance. "Betsey, too," I added softly, and concentrated on tying my laces.

She knew I wanted to talk. "When you care about someone and try to understand them, you often find things out about yourself, don't you?" She spoke in an offhand manner, but what she said was heavy.

"How did you know that?" My mother often astounded me with her insights.

"That's what being in love is all about." She mixed some tuna and soup together, as though she hadn't been talking about my innermost thoughts.

"Do you think I've changed?" I asked, wanting to take advantage of my mother's insights.

"I think your life has changed," she answered thoughtfully, "but you haven't. You've just become more yourself."

I thought a lot about what my mother had said. Betsey certainly had helped me discover things about myself that I didn't know existed. My talent for running was part of it. It made me appreciate the satisfaction that athletes enjoy when they perform, and I would never again ridicule them. Also, Betsey made me feel secure enough to shed my Lone Artist image. She had once accused me of hiding behind a paintbrush all my life, and she wasn't completely wrong.

More than ever I wanted to give something to Betsey. Since I had no previous experience with girls, I decided to consult Andy. After my mother went upstairs I dialed his number.

"What kind of present would Betsey like?" I began without even saying hello.

"Is it her birthday?"

"No, I just want to give her something special."

"Let's face it, Eric. I'm not an expert in the field of women, but I think you can't go wrong in giving her something connected with what you do best."

"I'm trying to narrow the field. Did you have something in mind?"

"You're an artist, remember?"

"You mean I should paint something for her."

"Your powers of deductive reasoning are extraordinary."

"That's a terrific idea. But what should I paint?"

"Eric, I've heard of writer's block, but this is the first time I've heard of artist's block. You've never been stumped before."

"It's for Betsey, don't you understand? It's got to be unique."

"Hey, I've got it!" he shouted.

"What?" I said impatiently.

"You," he roared. "That's the most unique thing I can think of."

"Me," I murmured.

"You," he repeated. "A self-portrait. Van Gogh did it, Rembrandt did it, why shouldn't Eric Wilson do it?"

"Isn't that pretty conceited?"

"Not with your mug, it isn't," Andy said, cracking up.

"Thanks a lot," I groaned.

"No kidding, you're the only person in the world who can do your self-portrait. Think about it."

"Hmmmmm," I hesitated. "Maybe you're right."

When I hung up, the idea became more and more appealing. I couldn't wait until dinner was over and I could go upstairs. I took the mirror that was over my dresser and propped it against the wall near my easel. Then I dug up some recent snapshots and studied them care-

fully. I knew from experience that my quick charcoal sketches were often the most successful, and I went right to work. It didn't take long for me to achieve a reasonable likeness, and then refine the shadings. It's always hard for me to be objective about my work, and the more I analyze it the more doubts I have. So I just slipped it into the back of my notebook and tried not to worry.

I know this sounds dumb, but I wanted to be in "our" park when I gave the sketch to Betsey. I wasn't about to bring the notebook with me in the morning, but when we were finished running and were sitting in our usual place, I arranged to meet her there later.

"I've never been here in the afternoon light," I remarked. "It must look so different."

"That's your artistic side showing," she said. "I never would have thought about that."

"Why don't you meet me here at five-thirty? I'll show you how light and shadow can create a mood."

"I'd like to," she agreed.

The park was very romantic in the late afternoon, or perhaps it just reflected my mood. There were a couple of mothers with baby carriages who were getting ready to leave, and an elderly couple were strolling back and forth when I arrived. Our bench was free and I sat down to wait for Betsey.

She appeared a few minutes later and sat

down next to me, sliding her arm through mine. I held her hand and looked into her eyes.

"It *is* different here at this time," she remarked, "but I have a feeling you didn't lure me here just to educate me about lighting effects."

"You're right," I told her. Then I momentarily had second thoughts about whether I'd done the right thing. Maybe she'd take it the wrong way, maybe think I was on an ego trip. Maybe I should have just bought her a bracelet with our names inscribed.

"You look so serious," she observed. "Is something wrong?"

"I hope not," I mumbled, and let go of her hand. I pulled the notebook out of my knapsack and balanced it across my knees.

"What is it?" she asked.

"It's something I want to give you, but I don't know if . . . if it's right, if I should . . . if . . ." My voice trailed off.

"Why don't you let me be the judge of that?"

"Here," I said, before I lost my nerve altogether. Then I slipped out the sketch and handed it to her.

She looked at it for so long that I finally had to break the silence. "Do you like it, Betsey? Tell me."

"Eric, Eric," she breathed, "It's the best present I ever got. It's very, very special."

And when she kissed me, I knew that Betsey Noble had been worth waiting for.

To read Betsey's side of this story, flip this book over and begin reading on page 1.